THEIR SECRETS REVEALED

B. A. CROSS

Editor: Heather Preis

Cover and interior book design: Lynessa Layne

Cover Photography: Alexi Lee Photography

Cover model: Kendyl Kerr

Paperback ISBN 979-8-9898689-0-2

eBook ISBN 979-8-9898689-1-9

FOR MY HUSBAND...

CHAPTER
1

THE YEAR IS 1907. LIFE IN LOUISIANA IS SUPPOSED TO BE SIMPLE. Farmers take care of their crops in the endless fields. Squirrels scurry underneath the monstrous, hundred year old, majestic oak trees. Gravel roads show the routes less traveled. Small groups of people shop in the nearest town to trade or hear local news. At the center of it all, there is family—a wholesome, loving unit that teaches the tasks of daily endeavors and gives support to raise hardworking people for hope of a promising future.

But yet, why does life seem so complicated?

Behind the façade of the beautiful oak trees and endless crop fields lies the mosquitos and termites that infest and destroy all that surrounds them. Feral animals reside inside the robust trees fighting for food to survive, along with the dead, foul ones that I can never seem to find. Pungent, sticky mud is trapped between each small, insignificant tiny rock that forms the beaten gravel road. Whispers carry into the streets from the gossip between the lowly townspeople.

I found that in the rubble is the path to discovering of how much one can take. Because how does one succeed if not pushed to the limits, to find out what someone is made of, and furthermore, what he or she is capable of: the good, the bad, the indescribable? A person may not be proud of these truths—the ones that keep us alive.

My name is Grace. I live here, in this estate with my father and mother. I am the sole heir to this strawberry plantation that has been in my family for two generations now. Our home is a stately two-story dwelling, sitting on hundreds of acres. It has a tall hedge garden to the left of the home with two century-old oaks flanking each side of the porch. Their towering presence casts a protective and serene ambiance over our familial domain.

When my mother gave birth to me twenty years ago, the doctor told her that she would no longer be able to bear any more children. Of course that broke my parents' hearts, knowing they would never have a son to pass along the DuBois surname. Thankfully, they never showed any disappointment in my inability to uphold the DuBois name when I marry.

When I marry. God...

I'm twenty years old, without a husband or even someone I could remotely call a suitor. Twenty is very old for this lifetime. By now, I should have a husband. Actually, I should *want* to have a husband and a plethora of children. Most women my age haven't wasted any time finding a man and producing heirs to their homesteads.

Predictable.

My stomach curdles inside just thinking about such old-fashioned conventions. I know I have more to this life than popping out babies one after the other. Maybe I feel this way because my mother did just fine with only having one child. I like to think I give my parents enough love for them to be satisfied with how life's events turned out for our family.

Well, most of the time.

I can't help it that I'm a little stubborn and strong-willed when I need to be. According to my mother, that is more often than she would like. I know I can take care of myself and our family business one day. I don't need a man and children to make me feel whole. I've been doing just fine so far. Society may view me as a fertile woman ready for production, but I have other plans. My priority is to take over the family plantation and the business that it encompasses.

It is known around the southern region that a beautiful maiden with long, wavy brunette hair and stormy blue eyes with a hefty dowry is still available.

That bothers me.

A fair share of families from surrounding towns travel to visit my home in hopes that I give their sons the opportunity to court me. But I like to take care of myself. I don't need a husband or a man to shelter and satisfy me. I can provide on my own account.

My father helped me become self-sufficient. He actually taught me more about being a man than what my mother would have liked. I can shoot pistols, smoke cigars, cuss, and do other rubbish in which a lady would otherwise not partake. After all, I am the son he was never able to have.

On the other hand, my mother taught me to read and write, uphold proper etiquette, and maintain the daily activities inside our house. She always hoped I would become a well-mannered lady who provided support for my future husband. It was clear how often I disappointed her, day in and day out, when I spent most of my time outdoors, tearing up my dresses and getting dirty performing tasks with the staff whom we employ.

Although my parents have different ideas for how they wanted to raise their daughter, one thing is certain—their love for me and each other. My parents' love for each other is so deep that nothing, even death, could break them apart. I see the way they look at each other across the dinner table when they don't think I pay attention. Sometimes, when they think I'm asleep upstairs, I sit on the steps and watch them slow dance in our living room to my father humming in my mother's ear as they hold each other close.

I cannot help that I have high expectations of marriage. I refuse for my marriage to be looked at as a transaction. There is more to uniting two business entities and then creating heirs to continue a loveless legacy. I can't stand knowing that a lucky schmuck will simply take my inheritance through vows of marriage just so he can one day call it his own.

My ancestors and I have worked too hard to learn the tricks of the trade. My grandfather built the two-story masterpiece we live in when he purchased the strawberry fields from a local farmer. The plantation became more of a success when my father started selling the strawberries to surrounding states by way of the railroad and eventually exporting them to other countries through New Orleans via the Gulf of Mexico. DuBois became more of a household name around the region thanks to my father. Eventually, the endless jobs of maintaining the strawberry plantations will be mine.

Or so I thought.

In the early hours one October morning, I suddenly awaken to the sound of shattering glass. I tentatively step into the hallway lined with our family photos, listening to find exactly where the noise came from.

There is a stillness in the air as I take a few breaths, trying to calm down. *Am I dreaming?*

I hear another window break downstairs. I panic and rush down the long corridor to my parents' bedroom on the other side of the second floor. While practically an adult, I like to be near them to feel safe. With the three of us together, we can be a stronger force and protect each other from whatever is happening.

A booming, foreign voice fills the silence, and I abruptly halt right outside of my parents' door. A tall, well-built man grabs my mom by her hair and drags her out of bed. He yells in her face, "Where is she?!" Then, I see a pistol in his hand with a finger already on the trigger. The look in my mother's eyes does not show an ounce of fear.

Actually, I see confidence behind her composed eyes as she looks up at the intruder. Her gaze doesn't give anything away.

Is he looking for me? Why? And where is my father?

I want to scream and divert the man's attention away from my mother, but something deep inside of me compels me to stay quiet. Maybe it's the way my mother protects me. From what, I don't know. Does she know? Regardless, I choose to keep my mouth shut.

I turn my head as I hear rustling downstairs on the main floor. Is there another intruder in the house? Is he fighting my father? My body can't seem to make any type of decision in either running to my father to aid him below or watching my mother with a crazy person holding a pistol. I freeze in a state of shock.

My eyes glue to the scene in front of me. When the stranger understands that my mother is not going to answer him, he points the pistol at her head without hesitation and pulls the trigger.

The gunshot jolts my body from its numb state. Now aware of my surroundings, it takes everything in me not to scream and run to my mother's falling body.

Suddenly I realize I don't have much time. I know I need to get the hell out of here before the cold-blooded stranger finds me and kills me too.

I turn from my spot to run when another gunshot fires downstairs on the main floor. *Father! No!* I want to go to him and check to see if he is hurt, but I can't risk my life. An eerie suspicion, a growing coldness, sweeps over me. I know my father can no longer help me.

For reasons I cannot understand, my parents sacrificed their lives to protect me. Whoever is trying to find me will get what they are looking for if I don't move. I can't let that happen.

My exit downstairs is compromised, so I turn toward my bedroom. My window is now the closest possible escape route from this uncanny set of circumstances.

The midnight sky bears a bright, full moon, which casts a haunting glow on the oak tree I need to reach quickly. If I get there in time, I can climb down and run to the tall hedge garden located on the side of our house. Maybe they won't be able to find me in there.

Whoever "they" are.

My mother loved the hedge garden when she wanted some alone time. When I would find her there, I would ask as a young child, "Why do you come here, mama?" She replied, "It blocks out life's noises, offering a quiet serenity. The tall hedges make me feel safe and secure. It offers me a time of reflection." Back then, it seemed silly and ridiculous to want to be alone, but right now, I can use some peace and serenity out of this fucked up situation. My mind and body need an escape, and that is just the place I can hide until the coast is clear.

As I cross the threshold to my room, I quickly look back down the hallway. The man who just murdered my mother comes out of my parents' bedroom, and we make eye contact.

"C'mere, bitch!" He sprints toward me.

Although I am fast from my experienced years of running in the strawberry fields when playing tag with my father or fellow plantation workers, I am no match for this stranger. His stature alone portrays his own type of daily physical maintenance. He snatches my ankle, and I smack my head as I fall to the hardwood floor. I try to kick his face with my heel, but he is too strong. He pins my feet down and climbs on top of me over my lavender silk pajamas.

"You Grace?"

I spit in his face, hoping to surprise him so I can squirm out of his hold. Unfortunately, that doesn't work. In fact, it just pisses him off more.

"Good nite, bitch."

The back of his pistol lifts up and comes down on my head. My world fades to black.

CHAPTER 2

I AWAKE LAYING IN A HORSE-DRAWN COACH. *WHERE AM I?* THE RIGHT side of my skull radiates pain. I try to touch at my throbbing head and notice I can't lift my hands. I feel an unpleasant constriction of thick fibers around my wrists. They are tied behind my back. My ankles are also bound together with rope. I'm restrained with nowhere to run.

Damn, what happened? Suddenly, the memories came back in a flash. I feel a surge of so much despair...and hate.

I look in front of me and see my perpetrator and his accomplice, the one who must have killed my father.

A sudden desire overcomes me to kill both of these goons with my bare hands. I try to wiggle out of my ties with so much force that the rope cuts into my wrists and ankles. I get nowhere. In fact, I think I made the bindings tighter, if that is even possible. I grunt out of frustration.

They laugh like they are watching some form of sick entertainment. *Bastards.*

My desire of killing them doesn't seem to become a reality any time soon, so I attempt to calm down and settle for asking some questions.

"Who are you?" I ask with a clipped tone.

The two men give me a hard stare. They seem angry, yet amused. I'm confused.

The man closest to my face is the one who captured me. He leans in slowly and responds, "Dat's none of ya concern." I didn't get a good look at him before, but now that I have nowhere to go, I take in this man's features with a little more detail. Surprisingly, he is older than I originally thought because he was so quick to catch me. He is bald, with dark brown eyes. His weathered skin meant he likely spent many of his days outdoors. His arms contain different types of markings—some areas covered in ink and some scars—but the dim morning light made it hard to tell the difference. A dirty, navy-blue bandana is wrapped about his skinny neck. *I wish I could choke him with it.* His tall, lean, and muscular stature gives him an advantage to annihilate anyone who comes in his way. And right now, that is me.

Our close proximity allows me to see the pure evil in his eyes. His hatred for me is so prominent that it emits off of his body like the heat waves coming off the ground in the middle of summer. I should be frightened of him and his accomplice, but my hatred for these assailants wins out on any anxiety I should be experiencing in this situation.

"It concerns me when you murdered my mother and father, asshole!"

"Oh, she's a lil' feisty one," the accomplice says. "He'll have some fun wit' her, I'm sho." The accomplice looks a bit less terrifying, compared to the devil's spawn next to him. His thick beard and burly stature makes me feel like he's only good for cutting down some trees. His hands contain scratches and calluses with dirt under his fingernails as they lay on his knees. He speaks with a slight country accent and a little humor behind his words. His tone is friendly, yet his words are anything but. I can't be foolish and let my guard down around him. He did just kill my father.

"Who is going to have fun with me?"

"Ya'll fin' out soon 'nough," the first man says with a sinister tone. His dialect is a little harder to understand. However, his point comes across through his demeanor. He seems to be the dominant one between the two.

Clearly, these two henchmen won't offer me any answers. I am frustrated, tired, and distressed, but showing my emotions will get me nowhere. Without knowing where I am or where I'm going, I decide to stay silent and allow myself to close my eyes and think about my parents. I have to stay strong for them. I owe it to them to keep moving forward. I need to preserve what little strength I feel like I have. I tell myself I cannot show any fear because these two are having fun torturing me with the unknowns.

My parents taught me strength in many different ways. When my grandfather died, I cried for days wishing for the good Lord to bring him back. He was the only other family member I had besides my mother and father. Although he was significantly older, I felt like he was the sibling I never had. After meals, he taught me card games in front of our fireplace or read me stories from his favorite books. He also taught me about business at a young age. I could always count on him to console me when I was mad at my parents for insignificant things.

During the funeral, I noticed my parents didn't shed a single tear. They maintained a stoic persona for all the other loved ones who mourned my grandfather's death. When my eyeballs finally stopped producing tears days later, one night, my mother tucked me into bed, and I asked why she and my father did not cry.

"Did you not love grandfather?" I bluntly asked her.

She looked at me with composure and said, "Your father and I loved your grandfather very much. We still love him. Though he may not be with us in body, he is still with us in spirit. He lived a fulfilling life here on Earth, and he will forever live a fulfilling life in Heaven.

Of course, we are saddened by his physical loss, but we rejoice in his eternal happiness."

I wanted to start crying again, but I had no tears left to shed.

My mother continued, "One day you will understand. Our love for family and each other go beyond this place. Our love and happiness are timeless. You need to stay strong for everyone else around you. One day, you will carry on without your father and me. Just remember, we will be with you always."

Remembering that my parents gave the ultimate sacrifice in trying to keep me safe, the most I could do is stay strong. I need to survive this and eventually figure out how to escape so their deaths are not in vain. I know they will somehow give me strength along the way.

I drift in and out of consciousness, unsure how much time passes. Suddenly, someone punches me in the stomach. The bald man sneers, "Git ready, bitch. We here."

I'm still laying in the coach with my wrists and ankles tied together, so I try to lift my head up as high as I can to peer out of the window. By this time, the sun is in the sky. On any other normal day, I would cherish the sun rising and the birds chirping while my father and I start our day maintaining the strawberry plantation.

Unfortunately, this is not any other normal day—the furthest possible, actually.

My eyes wander down back to earth, and my breath catches. The horse coach turns down a wide brick lane lined on both sides with oak trees. After a half-mile or so, the pathway ends in a complete circle that showcases a colossal estate. A monstrous plantation house is front and center.

This majestic pathway appears to be the only way in or out of the property.

Returning my attention to the focal point of the cul-de-sac, I take it all in. A pair of mirrored, curved staircases lead to the main-level entry doors of the white, three-story mansion. Large, almost floor-to-ceiling windows fill every level. Iron-fenced balconies wrap around the entire square house, and columns that start on the first level shoot all the way up to the base of the roof. Each window has beautiful tapestry that, of course, are open and arranged perfectly to give the perception that the people living here are meticulous and probably borderline conceited.

Symmetrical hedge gardens surround the house, each with a beautiful, round, multi-tiered travertine fountain depicting an array of creatures at the base. A seating bench sits in front of each fountain.

If my hands and ankles weren't currently bound together, I could imagine myself reading a book by the fountain while losing myself in the beauty of this magnificent place. Unfortunately, I know this place of serenity is just an illusion and has now become my prison.

CHAPTER
3

THE CARRIAGE, SURPRISINGLY, DOES NOT STOP AT THE FRONT OF the palatial house. We continue around the circular pathway along a dirt trail that curves around the hedge garden on the left side of the house.

"Where are we going? I thought you said we were here."

Before I can comprehend, Baldy back-hands me across the cheek. I don't want to give him the pleasure of hearing my pain, but I can't help the gasped sound that escapes my mouth from the surprise blow.

I don't understand what I could have done to these people to deserve such horrific treatment. I quickly realize it doesn't matter. I apparently have no privileges here or the right to talk to anyone.

The accomplice chuckles, not moving any ounce of his stout body to help me.

"Yo not to speek to me or anywun here. Got it?"

I don't want to respond to this savage for fear of another beating, but I figure I may receive another smack if I don't acknowledge what he just said either. I give a slight nod of my head in understanding.

I can practically feel my pulse in what feels like a hot handprint across my cheek, but I'm unable to touch my cheek or fix my long, brown hair that now covers my face from the force of the slap with my hands still tied together.

I don't deserve to be treated or talked to like this. For now, though, I'll be smart and pick my battles. I am outnumbered and tied up. There is nothing I can do. I must suck up my pride and save it for whatever comes next.

We finally pull around the hedge garden. I have to pee, and I am famished. It's late morning from where I can tell the sun rests in the sky.

The carriage coach stops in front of one of the many smaller cottages that reside on the property. This one is the least appealing, nestled, almost hidden from the rest of the estate, farthest away in the most western side of the property. I scan the rundown, unkempt conditions of this shack. Its weather-beaten exterior, once painted in a now-faded hue, peels away in uneven layers, revealing the tired, grayed wood beneath. The wooden planks, warped by years of exposure to the elements, seem to sag under the weight of memories and neglect. The roof, adorned with patches of rusty corrugated metal, bears the scars of countless storms, allowing sporadic beams of sunlight to infiltrate the interior. The windows are either missing or clouded with a film of grime, obscuring any view of the outside world. A solitary, tattered curtain, once a vibrant fabric, hangs by a thread, barely concealing the interior from prying eyes. Surrounded by a sea of overgrown weeds and tangled vines, the shack seems to shrink into its surroundings.

I wonder what happens over here.

It's a place to keep secrets. An unsettling pit forms in my stomach.

Do the owners of this estate know what these savages are doing? Would they help me if I escape?

Even if I escape, I don't have anyone to return to. My mother and father are gone. *I can't think like that.* I still have the plantation to maintain. I need to find a way out of here.

I miss my home and my parents. It saddens me that I'll never see them again. Grief springs tears in my eyes and closes my throat. But a resolve to survive, to honor my parents' sacrifice, and to take care of the employees that my parents hired for our strawberry business eases the pain as I adopt a stoic determination.

The man I currently despise the most in this world speaks to me, "Imma untie yer ankles. Ya betta not run, or I'll kill ya. Imma keep yer hands tied so ya don' do anythin' funny, ya hear?"

Again, with a minimal response, I give a slight nod.

"Good. Now, when I untie ya, ya clim' outta de carriage an' walk in de lil' cottage. Ya listen to what ya bein' told in 'ere."

I allow him to untie the rope around my ankles, fighting the urge to kick him in the face and sprint off at the first sign of freedom. By this time, his accomplice exits the back side of the carriage to guard it with his stout figure and make sure I don't have a change of heart and bolt.

I can't believe I am listening to this bastard's commands, but I know I have no other choice. These henchmen have me right where they want me.

As I enter the shambled cottage, I come face to face with a woman. I immediately have the urge to hate her as much as the men who brought me here, but her demeanor is different. Her head is cast downward, eyes looking down at her feet and hands clasping together at the front of her tattered dress. She looks…afraid.

"Don' let her outta yer sight. She'll run away, an' it'll be yer fault. Get 'er dressed an' fed an' I'll be back. Larsen'll keep watch ou'side this do' if she tries to escape. An' no talkin' to her. The less she know, the betta."

Ah, so one of these pricks is called Larsen. Maybe I can find out more information from this poor woman about this place. She seems harmless enough. Hopefully, she will help me.

After he slams the door, I know I don't have much time so I immediately ask the woman, "What the hell is going on?"

Her head snaps up, and she looks at me with dark brown eyes in shock.

"A lady don' talk like dat," she says. "And Imma no' suppose to talk to ya. I don' wanna get us in trouble."

This lady talks like the evil, bald man, yet she seems subordinate to him. How much authority does he have over her or others? He and his accomplice, Larsen, seem to perform similar tasks, but Baldy is definitely the one in control. Maybe I do need to worry more around this man than I originally thought.

She responded to my question without giving me a blow to my face, so I decide to keep talking. The more I know, I might gain an advantage and better my chances for a quick escape. I whisper, making sure Larsen doesn't hear us from his position right outside the door. "Please, I'm just trying to understand what I am doing here. I need to go home. I have responsibilities that need attention."

Instead of responding, she busies herself, gathering up what appears to be a long rag. She walks up to me and unties the rope around my wrists. "Put dis on," she says as she moves to another area of the cottage. "Imma sure ya have to pee beans that ya came from a long ways." She points to a hole in a wooden bench on the other side of the room.

If I didn't have to go so badly, I would tell her to shove the contents of what's in that hole right up her ass. Instead, I am relieved to have my hands at my own mercy and thankful for this kind soul. She's the only person I've seen who actually gives a hoot about other human beings around here.

"What's your name?"

At first, I think she won't answer. However, after a minute, she replies, "Ma names Hanna."

"It's nice to meet you, Hanna. My name is Grace."

She glances back at me, making sure I follow her previous directions to use the lavatory seat and dress in the cotton gown she set out that has no shape to it whatsoever. She turns around with a tray of bread, fruit, and water. The spread is nothing extravagant, of course, but enough to fill my hungry stomach.

I feel the need to ask more questions, but my famished state wins out. Plus, my previous attempts yielded only wasting my breath with neglected questions.

As soon as I finish the last bite of my meal, the door swings open, and the vile man appears once more. He grabs at my arm, "Git up. We leavin'."

He swiftly ushers me out of the doorway. Hanna calls out, "Will, she forgot 'em shoes!"

So the man's name is Will. Now I know both my captors' names.

I was so excited to eat that I didn't even notice I was given any shoes. Thankfully, Will allowed me to retrieve them before continuing north on foot with Larsen in tow.

CHAPTER
4

NORTH OF THE PROPERTY, IN THE FAR DISTANCE, A MASSIVE, wooded forest outlines the entire backside of the colossal estate. It appears to stretch out for miles, with an endless depth.

Hmm, I wonder if I get the chance to escape if I can hide in those woods. No one would find me in there.

Will and Larsen continue to bring me closer to the woods. The tension in the air grows thick between the three of us. Will has a tight grip on my arm, probably because he knows I'm unpredictable and at any real chance I can get, I will take down these assholes so they wish they never crossed me.

It's a trek from the cottage to the outline of the woods, and I carefully take in my surroundings.

During the brisk walk, I see five other cottages on the property, all in way better shape than the one I just left. There's a greenhouse on the other side of the estate behind the right hedge garden. In the middle, attached to the main house, is an enormous brick patio with multiple sets of furniture for dining and hosting events. At the very back is a massive octagonal gazebo that easily seats a large party.

I become lost in my thoughts of the multiple options for escape when we abruptly halt before entering the forest. Larsen steps forward and shuffles some dirt and leaves around the ground with his weathered boot. After a few minutes, to my surprise, he unearths two doors with a large, rusted, rectangular lock slipped through the handles attached to each door.

What is down there?

Larsen pulls out a key, unclasps and removes the bulky lock, and tries to open the doors.

The doors are heavy. Even with his stout stature, Larsen struggles. Eventually, he opens both doors but not without a sweat. *Great.* My chances of escaping are definitely becoming slim to none. The doors fall to the floor so hard that I can feel the ground shake underneath me.

The hole that we are all now staring into is pitch black. *Are they about to kick me down here? Is this it?*

Because I can't help myself, I ask a question. I might receive a smack in the face again, but I figure, what the hell. "Am I about to die?"

Will snickers, "Ya gonna wish yerself dead soon 'nough. But no, no' yet." I sigh a sense of relief even though his words are supposed to scare me. Of course I'm scared, but I now know I still have a sliver of hope too.

Larsen goes first into the hole. Steps lead to the unknown depths of this continuing nightmare. I feel like I am in Dante's *Inferno*. Which circle of hell will be my fate?

Will's grasp on my arm finally breaks free. "Follow 'em." I rub my arm, regaining feeling back into it, but by this time, I lose sight of Larsen. He descended so quickly ahead of me. *Obviously, they've been here before.*

I apprehensively take my first few steps down. It's pitch black. My sense of sight now gone allows for other senses to take over. I first register the warm, pungent air that hits my nostrils. The dampness of it intrudes my airways which, unfortunately, forces me to taste the god-awful odor. I cannot decipher what it reminds me of, but it is definitely unwelcoming.

I reach my right hand out and place it against the wall so I can descend with some stability. I may pass out from the smell. My soft hands feel a rough undulation of the wall mixed with some smooth surfaces in different forms of rock and stone. As my hand glides across the surface, a coating of clay and dirt soils my porcelain skin.

I hear something rustling around in the distance below me. I hope it's Larsen and not an animal that's about to eat me alive. I try to keep even breaths to slow my racing heart, but to no avail. *When will I reach the bottom?*

Just then, like someone heard my thoughts, a faint light appears at the bottom of the stairs, illuminating the rest of the way. With only a few steps remaining, Will kicks me down the rest of the way. My arms shoot out in front of me to catch myself. I am fast but not fast enough. My head smacks the ground, and Will laughs.

Bastard.

He'll have it coming to him one day. I'll figure out a way to pay him back.

He grabs me by my arms and stands me up before I can try to run or fight him. Standing behind me, he holds both of my arms behind my back. The smell of his hot breath in my ear makes me almost vomit.

"Ya gonna have a nice time down 'ere. I'll make sho of it."

Animals. Dead animals. That is the revolting familiar smell. I will never forget the odor of a rotting animal carcass. My family had multiple small sheds on our property, usually to store tools. More times than not, opossums, racoons, or other disgusting rodents found their way into the shed and couldn't get out. As soon as I opened the shed doors to retrieve a tool, I knew some animal had a slow, unfortunate death. My father made me find the carcass and remove it myself to teach me some type of life lesson. After two or three times, I persuaded one of our employees to remove it for me for extra pay. Sucker.

The damp smell, memories of dead animals, and Will's breath are literally about to make me puke when he turns to me, "If ya puke, I'll make sho ya the firs' ta go."

What the hell does that mean?

With Will at my back forcing my gaze in a certain direction, I swallow the chucks and look down a long underground tunnel. It is illuminated by a single row of lights hanging from the ceiling by hooks placed every couple of yards. The light bulbs are connected by copper wire, yet every other one is burnt out or flickering. The narrow tunnel only fits three people across, and the walls are made of various rocks, stones, clay, and dirt—exactly what my hands felt in the stairwell area.

It's eerie, like everything down here eventually dies. Feelings of despair begin to arise.

As my eyes continue to adjust to the new surroundings, I become aware that the tunnel contains wooden doors on either side of the void as we walk by.

Will and I continue until Larsen emerges from the other end holding yet another set of keys. He must have gone ahead to light the tunnel, as much as he could. The lightbulbs give off a dim setting, which only makes for a few yards of visibility at a time.

I notice each door has two small, metal covered openings—one at eye level with another at the bottom corner. What or *who* they keep behind these doors can be watched and fed from the outside world through these spaces.

We stop in front of what I now know is my door. Larsen unlocks the it with a key and pushes it open. When my new residence comes into view, Will shoves me from behind, and I fall to the cold floor.

"Enjoy yo stay, bitch."

Will slams the door, and the lock clicks back into place. Their footsteps grow fainter with each second. I glance around my enclosed jail cell. Four walls are lit by the faint lighting creeping in through the cracks around the door and small openings. I vaguely take in a blanket and pillow on the ground nearby.

My mind starts racing with the perils of my new reality. I take a few hyperventilating breaths while lying on the floor. Panic kicks in. I scurry to the door, get on my knees, and begin to bang on the door as loud as I can. My anxiety is crippling, and I yell with all of my energy. My hysteria engulfs all my senses as I pound on the door.

"Get me out of here! Don't leave me! Help! Help! Someone help me! Please!"

This scream for a few minutes until I hear a faint noise through my tantrum.

"Stop yelling, or they will come back and hurt you," someone says.

I instantly quiet from the shock of hearing another voice. Then, an overwhelming desire of company fills me. Now I understand I'm not the only one here. *Thank god!*

The voice adds, "They may not give you food either. So just stay silent."

I slam my whole body against the door, testing is stability, hoping it will magically open. When I realize that it won't, I slump against it. I barely move. "Who are you? What are we doing here?"

"Be quiet!" she chastises in a shouting whisper

I feel defeated. I finally allow myself to crumble. My hard exterior is broken, and I can't take anymore. I sink to the ground sobbing. I cry for myself. I cry for my mother and father. I cry for freedom.

CHAPTER
5

I CRIED SO MUCH THAT I DON'T REMEMBER FALLING ASLEEP. THE nightmare of Will and Larsen killing my parents and capturing me again woke me. Every time I close my eyes, my thoughts spin around and around like the famous merry-go-rounds I hear about in the papers at the trolley parks. Instead of enjoying the ride of the flying horses, however, I am haunted by the gory, catastrophic events that seem to never end.

What if I reacted differently back at my house? If I made a noise to startle Will, would my mother be alive? If I wasn't frozen by my parents' bedroom doorway, would I have moved sooner and escaped?

I know the answers to my questions. It wouldn't have made one bit of goddamn difference. But I can't help but wonder. It's driving me crazy.

To keep my sanity, I have to come to terms with my fate. I somehow must keep going. There is no way they will keep me down here forever. There must be a reason why they are keeping us.

Whoever *they* are.

I'm lost in my thoughts, again, because they are all I have, when a brisk knock comes at the door. As soon as I hear it, the sound is gone.

Hope rises in my chest, thinking I might get out of this hell hole sooner than I thought.

I wait for what feels like an eternity, but the sound of the lock unfastening doesn't follow.

Instead, I hear another noise from the bottom corner of the wooden door. A bowl slides across the ground through the metal covered opening that immediately shuts with a loud bang. I jump. For a split second, I wonder what is in the bowl. It's food.

I should be hungry. However, due to the circumstances and conditions of my captivity, I am not sure my appetite will ever return.

I must eat, or at least try. I need my strength for when I find a sliver of hope of leaving this place.

I grab the bowl and discover some form of stew, although it looks more like regurgitated meat and vegetables. Before I let my mind comprehend the nature of the substance, I place the bowl up to my mouth and drink it. *Ugh, this tastes like shit.* I cough as my tongue, throat, and stomach recoil in disgust.

I remember the first time my father made me swig his scotch to teach me a lesson about cussing. The foreign burning sensation of the liquor hit the back of my throat, coating all the way to my stomach.

My father didn't tell me how to drink properly, at first. I didn't know I was supposed to slowly enjoy the taste of the scotch, savoring the flavor. All he said was that a lady isn't supposed to cuss and to wash my mouth out of those dirty words.

My mother tried so hard to train me to be polite. But all I wanted was to be like my father. So he thought the best way to get me to stop cussing and deter me from alcohol was for me to take mouthfuls of scotch when I needed reminding. After all, I was supposed to be a lady.

Yeah right.

He figured out quickly I wasn't going to stop cussing. He might as well be the one to teach me how to drink correctly. After a while, the burning sensation and the tingling feeling became a warm comfort.

Now, if I could only imagine this horse shit was straight liquor, I could maybe keep it down and make it out here alive.

Another few days pass by. I track time based on the "food" service, usually with some sort of soup or stew, that comes three times a day, if I behave. We can easily eat without a fork or a spoon. I assume they don't want us to have weapons of any kind.

I don't blame them. I already attempted to keep my bowl they serve the slop in, just in case I could use that to my advantage somehow. Unfortunately, I discovered quickly that if I don't replace the bowl outside the metal opening soon after eating my food, a punishment is incurred.

There is a routine. A person comes by, knocks briskly one time, and slides the bowl through the metal opening. After we eat, we are supposed to slide the bowl back through the opening to be collected later. The unknown voice from my first night of my capture warned me to keep my mouth shut, but she neglected to explain the rules of giving back the bowl.

Bitch.

After I received my food for the third time, some of the shock had worn off. I had more time to process an escape any way I could. I thought I was smart when I chose to hide my bowl under my pillow. I honestly didn't know what to do with an empty bowl except maybe throw it at someone. At least it was something.

Not that long after I ate, I heard a noise right outside my door. Then keys rustled, and the lock to my door unclasped. An initial surge of excitement filled me to think I was possibly getting out of my until I saw the rage of the person in the threshold.

It wasn't Will or Larsen, but I couldn't make out his appearance in detail as he quickly rushed toward me.

How many people work in this operation?

The intruder grabbed me by the neck and pinned me against the hard wall. My head and back slammed against the uneven surface that dug into my skin.

His grotesque face contorted in anger, his breath reeked when he spoke with a strong accent.

"Where's yer bowl?"

I tried to respond, but I couldn't get the unspoken words out of my vocal cords. His callused hands squeezed around my neck. Then, he pointed a dirty finger right between my eyes.

"I said, where's yer bowl?!"

If he lowers his finger a little more, I'd bite that finger right off his hand. Instead, I dragged my arm up in the air and pointed toward my pillow and blanket on the ground.

He glanced over at my hiding spot and then looked back into my eyes.

"Ya think ya can get away wit' keepin' yer bowl?"

I had a hard time breathing with his hands still gripping my throat. I could not answer him.

"Do ya?!"

I shook my head no as best as I could. He released me, and without his hold, I fell to the floor, bending over to catch my breath. He walked irritably across the cell and lifted the pillow to retrieve the bowl. When he returned to my side, he commanded, "Git up."

I couldn't stand. I was still trying to breathe.

"I said git up!" He kicked me.

I fell over, grabbing my side when his heavy boot made contact with my rib cage.

"Yer weak, girl." He kicked me again.

I started to whimper. I told myself to bottle up my emotions, but this was too much.

"Yer cryin' for me now? I like it when ya cry for me." He continued to kick me.

"Aaahh!" I screamed. *God, this hurts so much!*

He crouched down low and close to my face. His hot breath almost fogged the air between us. "Nex' time, ya hide *my* bowl again, I'll come back in 'ere wit' a bat an' break yer bones. Do ya understan' me?"

I nodded my head yes. My ribs throbbed.

"Good."

He rose, left, and locked the door. I didn't receive any more meals that day.

After that moment, I knew this would be more difficult than I excepted. I know I have to play their game.

I need to keep my mouth shut and mind my own business.

CHAPTER
6

I START TO GO CRAZY. I AM LOCKED UP, I SMELL, AND I NEED HUMAN interaction. I'm losing my sense of time, but I think it's been four days. I would keep a tally if I could but I have no writing tool.

I stay quiet, only talking to myself since that first, *and only*, encounter with the voice from across the door. And my infamous bowl mistake.

I hope I never cross paths with that god awful human ever again. Although I yearn for companionship, lately it comes only by means of hate and torture. My health at this point is more important than trying to communicate to another prisoner. I opt for conversing with myself. It's safer that way.

"Help! Someone help me!"

Am I hearing someone? Or is that my imagination? Am I dreaming? Nothing. Moments pass in silence.

Yes, I am definitely going crazy. How do I get these voices out of my head? Perhaps I'm asleep, and my dreams are realistically vivid.

"No! Stop! Please!"

I grab my head and urge myself, "Wake up. These voices are not real. Just wake up."

The female voice gets louder. "Help!"

"Git that bitch to stay quiet, Larsen."

Will?

"She's squirming too much. Hold her down."

"Don' put ya hand on 'er mouth, or she'll bite ya."

Maybe this is real.

Noises scuffle outside my door. I want to rush to it and say something, but I don't. I'm afraid of what they will do to me.

"Here, use this," Larsen says.

"No! Stop!" cries the female voice one last time.

Smack! Clank!

Silence.

"God, Will. Did ya kill 'er?"

"No, I shut 'er up like what ya should 'ave done. Now drag 'er in that room ove' there."

Bastards.

Who is that girl? Is she like me? Was she forced to leave a family and life behind? One in which we will never return?

Stop talking like that. Yes, I will make it back!

I hear a wooden door slam shut, and Will and Larsen's footsteps walk back to the direction of the stairs, at least from what I remember. It's been so long now.

I begin to wonder how Will and Larsen fit in with this ploy. They capture us and bring us prisoners here to this dungeon, and then "others" give us food. Will and Larsen must be lackeys to someone who doesn't want to dirty their hands.

Whoever it is will need to watch their backs. One day, I will find my revenge.

Another noise—one I've heard before—distracts me. The flap in the bottom of my metal door opens and in comes my food. Red beans.

My heart races, and I welcome the change of pace. My stomach performs somersaults, excited to eat a familiar dish. My hands tremble. I know this meal, and I know the day of the week.

Today is Monday.

This little piece of information gives me a bite of reality to the outside world. It perks my depressive mood and allows me to concentrate on facts beyond that poor girl and the mastermind of this scheme.

I raise the bowl to my nose slowly and deeply inhale the smell of the beans. I immediately think of my mother and our Mondays together tending to the laundry. Laundry days are long so dinner preparations were simple. Red beans is an easy meal to cook and requires little attention—the perfect Monday dinner.

My mother and I spent most of the day handwashing the laundry and hanging the clothes and sheets on the drying line. I snuck away and stirred the beans every once and awhile. Sometimes I forgot to soak the beans the day before. Then, instead of red beans on Monday, we had to fend for ourselves to survive until Tuesday.

Now, in this hell hole, unfortunately, every day meant surviving for the next day.

I bring the bowl slowly to my dry, cracked lips and savor the taste of the beans as well as the bittersweet memories it stirs in my mind. For the first time since being here, I do not want to finish this serving of food. I want to hold onto the memories of my mother and I, outside with the wind in our hair while we hang the laundry and eat a hot, nourishing meal.

I slowly place the empty bowl back through the opening and gently close the little metal door. I bite my lip as it begins to quiver, trying to hold it together, but I start to cry all over again.

I crawl back to my tattered pillow and blanket with tears in my eyes. I lay down and think about the outside world. I close my eyes and draw the memory back. I remember being mad about having to help her all day on Mondays. Laundry is a chore for the ladies of the house to perform every week. I always preferred to work in the fields with my father.

I remember my mother's smile on those days. She cherished those Mondays because she knew I had to spend time with her. At every chance, she corrected my posture and foul-mouthed habits.

Those days brought me so much grief at the time and now bring me joy through my current despair. I want to go back and tell my mother how much I love and appreciate her.

But I can't.

My thoughts turn to the mysterious inhabitants at the main house, doing laundry and cooking red beans. I feel sure there is no love in the house or at this estate. The owners probably don't even do their own laundry. They probably sit and bicker at one another about money and wealth.

I hope they are unhappy. The hatred inside me wants them all to suffer.

One day, they will.

The following day, food service does not come.

Just when I start to figure out the routine, my sense of time warps again.

Great.

Time is my gate keeper. It maintains my sanity. It serves as my reference point, the only one I can have down here.

There is no sunlight to help the situation. I sit in almost darkness, except for the flickering of lights that barely illuminate the long hallway outside these wooden doors. I catch a glimpse of that single light through the cracks of the door or when the top metal opening opens briefly.

The "others," or guards I now call them, keep watch of us down here. I guess they need to verify we are still alive from time to time. I cannot see their whole faces, but different pairs of eyes check on me a couple of times a day. Some look shorter than others, some have facial hair, some have dark skin, and some are fair skinned. They must rotate on shifts, making sure us prisoners don't escape or harm themselves. There isn't much we can do given our circumstances.

These conditions are grueling. I like to think I am brave and strong. However, given the lack of food and inhumane punishments, anyone could easily sway on the verge of breaking.

But I won't let them win. I can't.

This cell tests my mental and physical abilities. It reminds me of one of my favorite childhood games—hide-and-seek. When I was about seven years old, I asked one of the servants in the strawberry fields to play with me. He was a little hesitant at first because he was supposed to be working.

We had played this game before and were scolded by my father when he caught the servant failing to fulfill his daily duties. Then my father chided me to stop disrupting the laboring activities required to run the family business smoothly.

So when I asked him to play hide-and-seek with me again a few weeks later, the poor servant didn't want to get me or himself in trouble. Looking back, I should have listened to him.

I was very convincing, even at my young age, in persuading him to quickly play a round with me. He hid first.

I slowly counted to twenty because the fields were vast. The servant needed some time to find a hiding place. After I finished counting, I ran to his usual spot. An oak tree on the side of the strawberry crops was wide enough to hide at least three people behind it. I raced to the tree, knowing he was there.

That was too easy.

I wasn't satisfied and wanted to find a hiding spot better than that one.

The servant started to count, and I ran as fast as I could to the small cottage on the property not far from the fields. It housed tools needed to plant and harvest the strawberries. I found a small cabinet to hide in and waited.

My heart beat so fast. This was my favorite part—my turn to hide. I liked outsmarting people, even back then. I liked the chase and the adrenaline rush. But this time, I waited a long time, longer than usual.

I knew my hiding spot was a good one so I figured he needed some time to find me. Enclosed in that small, dark space, just waiting to come out, I lost track of time.

I began to wonder, do I come out and give up? Then I stopped thinking about the game, and my stomach growled with hunger. Should I go home and eat dinner? I needed to urinate. Do I stay in here and go on myself?

The seconds turned into minutes, and the minutes turned into hours.

I wasn't ready to quit yet. Surely, someone would come looking for me. I had to win the game.

I learned later, the servant was interrupted by my father, wondering why he was counting behind the tree. The servant didn't want to get us both in trouble so he made the excuse of needing to urinate behind the tree.

Then he forgot about me. No one came to look for me. Little did he and my father know, I waited so long in the dark, tiny space that I missed supper that night and piddled on myself, twice.

Finally, when I didn't arrive for supper that night, my parents decided to search for me. I eventually heard my father's voice in the cottage yelling my name. Only then did I abandon my hiding spot. I was so hungry.

My father hugged me tightly and asked me what the hell I was doing in the cabinet. That was the first time I heard him swear. I explained I was hiding in a good spot, and I didn't want to give up.

This dark, underground cell brings back that memory. I am losing my sense of time. I also know I am in another very good hiding spot. It is so good that no one will come looking for me again.

I have to escape on my own.

CHAPTER
7

THE OUTSIDE WORLD RUMBLES ABOVE ME. NOISES OF VARIOUS intensities drowns out the silence and deafens my ears. The small, flickering lights outside my door in this underground hell hole swirl in waves across my rock walls.

"What is happening?" a prisoner bravely asks.

"I don't know, but you need to stay quiet!" exclaims someone else. *Here we go again.*

I can't determine how many people are down here with me. Their voices all sound similar behind these wooden doors. I think there may be about three or four other people besides me.

Sometimes an adventurous soul stirs up the courage to speak without having any idea if Will, Larsen, or another guard watch us, just waiting to beat us when we start to talk. Then, a voice of reason tries to shut it down quickly to avoid all of us taking the fall for someone else's stupidity.

I embrace the entertainment. I have yet to partake in the so-called mini conversations. This time, though, I think I will. I wait my turn, just in case a guard arrives, hearing our pathetic encounters. More white noise hums louder.

"Seriously, what i- is that sou- sound?" the first voice yells, clearly not satisfied with staying quiet. Her voice quivers with fear.

"Would you just be quiet for once before getting us all in trouble!" the second voice yells in frustration.

CRACK! BOOM!

A loud clap splinters the air above us, followed by a heavy rumble.

"Ahhhhh!" Multiple prisoners shriek in unison. More piercing sights and sounds flicker, snap, and subside, and more voices yell.

"I'm scared! Is anyone else scared too?" another prisoner asks.

No one is coming to check on us in this weather, so I decide to talk. "No." I try to reply with confidence, but my unused voice is hoarse.

"Why? Why aren't you scared?" the unknown voice continues to ask.

"Because it is just a bad thunderstorm," I say with more umph behind my words. My tone is sharp and curt, yet I don't really care. They can't see my face anyway to know who I am. I know this is more than a severe thunderstorm. The other women don't seem knowledgeable about the weather patterns in this region of the south. I have a suspicion that they aren't familiar with hurricanes.

And that's exactly what this is—a hurricane. The wind howls, along with heavy bands of rain, lightning, and thunder. It must be right over us. Yep, no one is coming toward us, not to offer food nor punishment.

Great, another day or two of not eating.

I sit against the wall closest to the sounds of the thunderstorm outside and welcome the unexpected weather. Not that long ago, I would have been petrified just like the rest of the other inmates here. The last hurricane came close to Ponchatoula only about a month or two ago.

When my father and I were in the fields that day, the clouds in the sky indicated some bad weather on the horizon. We followed our usual protocol.

We finished our chores in the fields and moved all the lightweight and loose items into either the little cottage on the property or in the main house. Sometimes, if we had enough time, we tied some of the heavier items to an oak tree in case a tornado accompanied the hurricane.

That's the scary part with hurricanes. Although there is enough time to prepare for the bad weather, the tornados that develop within them are unpredictable and deadly. Underground is the safest place to be. Unfortunately, in Louisiana, most areas do not have an underground. Usually, the soil is too wet to make a hole or ditch deep enough to keep a family safe from such a storm.

Funny, now I am safer underground in this weather than in the outside world. This illusion of safety, even for a few hours, brings comfort and happiness. Lucky for me and everyone else down here, we have a better chance of survival than those assholes above ground.

Good riddance.

Throughout the night, the rain, thunder, lightning, and screams continued.

I remember my mother used to pull out candles and light them when the skies turned really dark. We ate dinner in silence, listening to the sounds of the storm, making sure we didn't hear a tree fall or other types of damage around the property.

For some reason, hurricanes always seemed to pass over during the middle of the night. My mother tucked me into bed, and I made sure to pull the covers over my head.

"Don't be scared, my Grace." My mother tried to soothe me.

"Why aren't you scared?" I asked. I always wondered why she stayed so calm during a storm.

"Because I'm with you. We are together. Nothing will break us apart, not even a storm."

"But I don't want us to die."

"We won't, sweetheart."

"But one day we will, right?"

"When we are supposed to."

"How do you know when you're supposed to? I thought it just happens."

"You're right, but deep down inside, you will know when it's your time. And I can tell you, it's not your time or mine. We are fine, ok?"

"I guess."

"Go to sleep, my child."

"But, momma, I can't. The rain is too loud."

"Do you know what it means when it rains?"

"No."

"When it rains, it means an angel received his or her wings. The heavens are celebrating."

"Really?"

"Yes. So you see, the rain actually tells us that it is a happy time. There is nothing to fear. Sometimes, they just celebrate a little too loudly."

She squeezed my hand tightly and kissed me on the forehead.

"Good night, my Grace."

"Good night, momma." I fell asleep before she left my room.

I know my mother accepted her fate when Will pointed the gun at her head that night. I'm sure my father did too. Hearing the rain tonight soothes me. I envision my parents receiving their wings together in heaven. I picture how happy they are as heaven rejoices.

I fall fast asleep.

CHAPTER
8

I WAKE UP TO A FAMILIAR SOUND OF THE LITTLE METAL OPENING presenting my first mystery food of the day. Thank God because I am starving!

The storm finally passed sometime during the night.

I finish eating when the lock on my door jiggles. Full of sudden, nervous adrenaline I grab my empty bowl and scurry to the back corner of my prison cell. My heartbeat pounds in my ears.

What do I do? What are they about to do to me?

No one has touched the lock in a long time, so I have no idea what this means. I look around me like I can grab another weapon to protect myself but realize all I have is this stupid bowl. *Like that will do anything.*

The door opens, and I raise my bowl with my right hand as if to throw it at the intruder. Just my luck, the guard from the other day who strangled me, *or maybe it was a week ago now*, breaches the doorway.

Shit.

I take a better look at him as he stands at a distance. He is average height for a man and a little overweight. His skin is tan and leathered, and his face and hands are dirty, like he works outside in the fields all day every day. His confident stance in the doorway, the righteous tilt of his chin, and the hardness of his eyes portray him to be nothing short of an asshole.

He holds a pistol pointed right at me. He doesn't move. I don't even breathe, thinking he may pull the trigger just for the hell of it.

He smiles, and bile creeps up my throat. His eyes undress me through my thin, tattered gown. I cringe. We face off for about a minute, unmoving. Then, another man enters my cell.

No! Not two of them. I definitely can't fight off two of them.

Before more dark and unwelcoming thoughts continue, the second guard speaks clearly and confidently, "Put down the bowl and stand still."

"Ya betta be careful wit' this one. She's a wil' one, sir," says the guard with the pistol.

The second guard approaches me slowly. Just when I thought he might be my savior, I begin to worry about his intentions too. He is taller and more muscular than his accomplice. He sports a short beard and mustache. He appears better groomed, like he actually bathed within the last week and cares about his appearance.

"Is that so?" he asks, stopping right in front of me. He never takes his eyes off me. His stare pierces me, but I don't shut my eyes. Instead, I look past him toward the doorway, where I wish I could run and escape.

The grotesque guard keeps his pistol steady on me, while the one in front of me holds out a thick, rough, piece of rope. I say a prayer in my head, hoping they aren't planning to take what little is left of me.

I follow his directions and set the bowl at my feet. I try not to touch the guard in front of me and accidently give him any wrong ideas.

"Give me your hands," he demands. I swallow my disgust and pride and slowly stick my hands out together. All I want is to knee him in the ballocks and punch his face, just like my father taught me years ago to defend myself. On the other hand, I want to show compliance, that I am not a threat, for now. I don't feel like being man-handled at the current moment, nor do I have the energy to fight back.

His face transforms with a perverse smirk that makes my stomach sour. "Good girl," he patronizes. *Gross.* The guard with the weapon snorts.

I lower my eyes because I can't stand the sight of either of them.

He ties the rope around my wrists, linking them together tightly before grabbing my chin and forcing me to look at him. "Follow me." Just as quickly as he entered the room, he leads the way out.

I release a breath that I didn't realize I held. The guard wiggles his pistol to get me to move. Just as directed, I walk out of my cell with the weapon pointed at my back.

We head through the tunnel and reach the bottom of the infamous steps that led to my dungeon of doom. Now, they feel like my lift toward heaven, reminiscent of Dante's *Paradiso*. No amount of adrenaline is a match for these steps that seem to grow tenfold as I climb each one. My legs are sandbags after days cooped below.

The guard behind me shoves the pistol into my back. "Hurry up, girl!"

I want to tell him to shut the hell up, but I am just glad for the chance to get out. The heavy doors at the top are already open, and the sun's heat beams on my face. My eyes water, trying to adjust to the new brightness. I can't tell if it's from my euphoric state or the change in lighting, but I inform myself not to fall on the final steps leading upward as my vision eventually clears.

This is really happening!

We climb out of the hole and walk a few paces before I realize that we aren't alone. Two lines of people stand in front of us. They are strategically placed in a double row facing each other as my guard escorts me through them. I feel like I'm in a gauntlet, preparing to fight for my life.

They just stand there like statues, staring at me silently as I walk through them. These must be the other guards who checked on us from time to time. Although they appear unarmed, they still emit an aura of power around them, like they can squash me at any time to prove who is in charge. Their number unnerves me. Knowing there is such a presence reduces my chances of escaping, again.

Far in the distance, butlers and maids scurry around the brick patio. Two people sit at a table in the massive gazebo. They eat patiently while a half dozen servants tend to them. I immediately hate them, all of them, especially the two acting like it's just another day on the plantation.

Do any of them realize what is going on underground and how we are treated like dogs?

They sit too far away for my eyes to distinguish any kind of detail, except one is a man and the other a woman. They have to be the ones responsible for all this. Whatever *this* is.

The guard behind me and I continue until we reach the end of the gauntlet. *Finally.* He halts, causing me to pause with him. I do not know where the other guard went. I lost track of him when I first came out of the hole, too distracted by everything and everyone else surrounding me.

We turn to face the double row of servants and wait. I stare down the void that exists between the two rows of guards. No one talks. No one moves. We continue to wait. For what, I have no idea.

Then, another guard emerges from the hole with his prisoner. I knew there were others down there, but I'm surprised that this prisoner is a man. I thought we were all female. I wondered if we were being trafficked and sold off as wives, prostitutes, or God knows what else. Clearly, I was wrong.

Then, what the hell am I doing here? What the hell is he *doing here?*

As the male prisoner approaches me, his face holds confusion and surprise, mirroring my own. He is tall, probably close to six feet, and he is quite handsome. At least he was before being thrown into the same conditions. *Has he been here longer than me?* Who knows.

His clothes are tattered like mine. Instead of a gown, his garment is a pair of loose-fitting slacks and an oversized shirt. Both contain holes and ripped seams in various spots. His growing facial hair and full head of brown hair are dirty and unkempt, and his green eyes take me in, as I do him. His wrists are also tied together by rope. They place him to stand next to me.

I want to speak to him so badly, but the army of guards will gladly take turns torturing me for talking. Before I can imagine what I would say, though, another guard and prisoner exit the hole. A female, dressed with my same attire, gazes around with jerky motions and cowers into herself as she is pulled along.

She sees me and the man to my side and immediately casts her head down, like she shouldn't be looking. She likely won't survive much longer. The poor girl seems fearful of everything, even life.

One by one, more guards and more prisoners arise out of the hole. In all, there are twelve of us—eight males and four females. We are all teenagers or young adults. Some appear petrified, while others appear unfazed. I understand the lack of emotion because why give these assholes the satisfaction of fear?

The guard who tied my wrists returns and addresses group, "Prisoners, you all have been brought here for a special purpose. You may not understand the reason now, but eventually it will be revealed to you. During your stay here, you will be required to perform certain tasks and follow directions without any remarks or resistance. If you speak when you are not spoken to, or oppose any instructions, then there will be consequences."

My mind whirls with confirmed suspicions, and hope dwindles as I contemplate the reality of never returning to the world I once knew. With no escape in sight, I die a little more inside, if that's even possible.

We have a purpose?

The man continues to speak loudly so all of us can hear him, "Your main task during your stay is to play a game. This is a game of strength and wits. There will only be one winner. "

A game? I'm supposed to play a fucking game?

"Other objectives may present during your stay that you will also need to complete without question, but your end goal is to find this flag."

He raises a bright orange, rectangular flag attached to a small stick above his head. *Great, so our purpose is to find a flag? None of this makes any sense.*

"This flag is already hidden somewhere in these woods behind us. You are not allowed to go beyond these woods. There is a perimeter of barbed wire that will keep you contained within the game area. You all are to return to this spot before the sun sets so we can bring you back to your cell. Anyone that does not return will be hunted down and killed. Finally, don't try to leave. Any attempt to escape will be grounds for immediate execution. That does not only stand for the game but any time during your stay."

The woods behind us appear endless. God knows what creatures reside in there. Upon my arrival, the forest was my escape route, but now, I can't help but feel like the woods are where I'm supposed to die. But I must be the one to win, for my family. Maybe the winner will be able to leave? *Yeah right. They will never let us go.*

Just as the question populates in my head, one of the teenage boys asks, "What does the winner actually win?" The guard stalks down the prisoner line to stand in front of him. The boy trembles with the knowledge of his error.

The guard slaps the boy's face and shouts, "That is a warning! Did I say you have the right to speak? No one here has the right to say anything!"

I find myself still appalled by this treatment for simply asking a valid question. We *do* have rights! We are human beings. I want to argue. I want to give him a piece of my mind. This whole charade is stupid. I scream in my mind, *Treat us with respect and stop abusing us. Give us real food and let us use a goddamn bathroom.*

The guard makes eye contact with me. Can he tell I was shooting daggers at him through my eyeballs? He walks slowly with his fists still balled by his sides. As he approaches, he must sense my hatred. He says, "You seem rather angry. Would you like to say something, too?" He stares at me with returned hatred and such dark brown eyes that they appear as black as night.

I hold my head high to simulate a lack of intimidation. Unfortunately, I know I should follow his directions and bite my tongue. So I choose to stay silent. I would love to spit in his face.

He chuckles with a low sinister laugh, "That's what I thought."

He signals to the other men, and we are all turned to face the woods. As he unties the rope from my hands, he smirks again. "Good luck, sweet girl. Don't let the wildlife get you."

He releases me into the unknown.

CHAPTER
9

I SLOWLY START TO WALK INTO THE WOODS. THE UNKNOWN PIQUES my curiosity, but I know I need to be cautious. This seems too good to be true in some ways. I'm not locked or tied up, and guards are not dragging me around by my arm. Yet, I can't shake the feeling that this game doesn't make any sense.

Other prisoners decide to sprint full speed ahead probably thinking they will be the first one to find the flag or distance themselves from the guards and our entrapment. I don't blame them.

I want to talk to the other prisoners and see if we can work together on a strategy of escape, but I want to wait so we are out of ear shot of the guards. The ones who sprinted off are too far away to call out to by now, and the ones who stayed behind appear so scared that they will likely be more of a crutch than a help.

I begin to settle for a solo game strategy when I hear a voice.

"Hello," a soft, comforting greeting turns my head. It feels so pleasant to hear words other than "bitch" or some kind of command. The handsome, green-eyed man looks at me expectantly.

"Hello," I reply weakly. I clear my throat to try to stimulate my vocal cords. He is definitely easy on the eyes, but my time here has made me suspicious. I wonder about his intentions.

"My name is Charles."

"I'm Grace."

He reaches out to shake my hand. But I hesitate. What used to be such a simple gesture of kindness now seems like a luxury or a false pretense. I have been manhandled too many times already since my capture, and I feel as though I can't trust anyone. Can I?

"It's ok. I won't hurt you," Charles assures me, witnessing my internal battle.

I release an audible sigh of relief and return the handshake. His hands are rough. He must work in the fields. They remind me of my father's hands. I'm curious about his life before all this.

"Where are you from, Grace?"

"Ponchatoula."

I offer as little information as possible. Should we even be wasting these precious moments when we could be searching for the stupid flag? I continue to walk slowly, hoping he will follow.

Any fear or purpose for this temporary freedom is outweighed by the joy of speaking with another person, especially one so nice. "You?"

Charles matches pace with me. "Houma. Have you been here long?"

"A week or more, I think." My voice strengthens with every word, as does my confidence.

"Wow! I've only been here about four days." *Four days.* It doesn't seem like a long time, but when every day goes on forever, it feels like a lifetime. I have lived two lifetimes compared to Charles. "You've survived here a lot longer than me."

I swallow any answer, unsure how to respond. We are both survivors in my mind.

"I can tell you're strong, not easy to break. I hope you've been giving everyone hell in there." He chuckles.

He's trying to ease my mind with his jovial nature. I have to admit, it's working. I crack a small smile, not the kind that shows any teeth. This whole situation isn't that funny.

Who can I trust here?

Is it better to be alone? I have spent a lifetime in darkness already. My body aches for human interaction but my head is skeptical of everyone.

"Hey over there!" someone shouts our way. Another man jogs over to us. He is bigger and thicker than Charles. "Do you want to team up with me?" he asks Charles.

Charles glances at me. We can work with other people to achieve our end goal faster. I nod slightly to his silent question. Looking back at the newcomer, Charles says, "Sure. We were just saying that the more numbers we have, the better chances we have to find the flag."

The man looks over at me with confusion and perhaps something a bit more sinister. "No, I meant just you and me. She will only slow us down."

My fists curl at my sides. I am about to strut right over to him and punch his ugly face when Charles blurts out with confidence, "Absolutely not."

The newcomer takes a step closer to Charles, leaning in as if to conspire, "C'mon. You know we'd do a way better job at finding that flag if you and I stick together. She's a girl. What would she have to offer anyway. Girls are good for one thing only—being domesticated. She wouldn't make it one day in these woods."

Bastard.

My feet move of their own accord toward this low life. My fists are still clenched so tight that I have lost circulation in my hands. My cheeks burns with untapped rage.

Suddenly, an arm crosses my midsection. Charles curls his body around mine and addresses the man once more, "No."

Is he talking to me? I look up at his face, but he isn't watching me. He stares at the newcomer, the directness of his gaze equal emphasis to his response.

The man hesitates, dumbfounded, and then shrugs his shoulders. "Your loss," he snickers before running off. When the man is safely out of sight, Charles turns to walk the other direction. I resume my place beside him.

"Why did you do that?" I ask Charles.

"You're a lot stronger than he is. We'd make a better team."

"I was ready to punch him, but you held me back."

"I know. But you can't make yourself a target already. And you can't hurt yourself. We need our strength for anything more serious that will happen soon."

"I would have taken him out, you know," I defend.

He smiles. "I have no doubt about that."

We continue to wander silently in an unknown direction. The trees are sky high and spaced a few yards away from each other, making it hard to determine any orientation to where we are. The sun tries to beam through the leaves onto the swampy terrain, but it doesn't quite get there. Most of the ground is brown and mushy from heavy rain and winds from the hurricane we all heard the night before. Tree limbs, branches, and leaves scatter the ground. I keep looking down at the ground to pay attention that I don't trip or step in a big slushy puddle. Although I have shoes on that were provided back in the rundown cottage, there isn't much to the thin material.

I try to breathe in through the humid air while I ponder at what just happened. I wish I could have punched that asshole. I wanted to regain some of the strength I've lost as well as some of my sanity. My physical weakness makes me mentally weak. I need to regain control somehow, after these people took everything from me.

"How were you taken?" Charles's timber interrupts my inner thoughts.

My steps falter out of sync. His question spurs the cycle of memories. As prevalent as they are, being my only companion these days, I am not ready to answer him. Tears sting the back of my eyes, and I avoid his gaze. Even if I can trust Charles, I don't want to show signs of weakness, no matter how hard. I adopt a more confident stride, in hopes it will mask how unsteady I feel inside.

"I wish not to answer."

He increases his own pace to catch up to me and leans in slightly. "I'm sorry. I don't mean to upset you. If it makes you feel any better, I'll answer that question for myself. I was taken inside my own home. I had just come back inside from harvesting my rice. Someone was waiting for me inside the house. I didn't even know what happened. I was hit over the head and blacked out. When I woke up, I was in a carriage that brought me here."

Charles didn't hesitate to share his story, like he accepted his fate. I too want to show strength through despair, but I couldn't fully accept what happened, at least not my parent's death. I want to go home.

"Do you miss home?" I timidly ask. I'm sure he left more than his rice farm behind.

"Yes, every second that I'm here. I wonder who is taking care of the rice farm while I'm gone."

"Do you have any family?" I don't know what compels me to ask when I clearly won't share my own answers. Yet, I want to know if there is a possibility his parents or other family members were killed like mine.

"I actually live by myself, but I have a lot of workers who help me care for my land. My mother died while in childbirth with me. And my father died last year from typhoid fever. I've been on my own ever since."

"No wife or kids?" I internally slap myself. Why did I ask that question?

"No, not yet. I'm only twenty-one. I still have time. Maybe one day, if we ever get out of here," he says with a smirk. We walk quietly side by side, taking in our surroundings without clear intention. We approach a broken tree trunk laying on the ground. Charles is the first to climb on top of the sideways trunk. He reaches out his hand for me to grab as he helps me find my footing to climb the trunk also. We both stand on top of the tree for a brief moment, and Charles is slow to let go of my hand. My heart begins to beat faster. *Why does he have this effect on me?*

"How old are you?" he eventually asks as he jumps off the broken trunk.

I follow his lead and jump off too. "I'm twenty." I hold back more personal details about the family life that I unwillingly left back home, and I am relieved when Charles doesn't press me.

We come upon another fallen tree, and Charles sits on it. "Well, what do you think the hell is going on here? I tried to come up with reasons, and I can't seem to formulate any explanation." For such a loaded question, his posture is relaxed. He flails his arms around like he's introducing me to the forest himself. His demeanor is disarming. I like it, but I remind myself not to get too attached, for many reasons.

"I don't know either. I spent days considering it and then decided it doesn't matter why I'm here. All I want to know is how to get out."

"Maybe we can work together," Charles casually offers.

Again, the battle between hope and suspicion, keeping an open mind and protecting myself, wars inside me. Working together should mean better success. Right?

"Sounds good to me."

Charles smiles wider, and it lights up his face. His boyish grin makes him even more handsome than before. He hops up from his seated position. "So, where do we start?"

"I honestly have no idea, but I have a feeling that no one is going to find that flag today."

Charles quirks his head quizzically.

I explain myself, "The guard said that when it gets dark, we need to return back to the hole. I figure this might take a while. So day by day, I was planning to scope out the land and see if I find any clues. Also, I figured we weren't eating lunch today so we may need to find some food while we're at it."

Charles nods as he looks around us.

There is no wildlife to be found around here. The hurricane probably scared them all off. All that remains to be seen are wet, broken tree limbs and leaves scattered all over the ground. The shadows that cast off from the trees allow me to tell that the sun has crossed over the midline and is beginning to make its descent.

"I'm a little worried that if the guards think we are collaborating, they may sabotage us somehow. So maybe when we go back, we should arrive at different times or come from different directions so we don't look suspicious."

"But they said that there are no rules, except escaping. We should be okay," he counters.

"I beg to differ."

Charles turns back to me, looking directly in my eyes, trying to interpret the words I leave unsaid. I hope being part of a team doesn't hold me back. I know it is hard to trust each other, but some common sense needs to be addressed here.

"They said there are no rules, but it's a two way street. We may do whatever we want, except escape, but they can do whatever they want, too. I'm sure of it."

Charles' jaw drops open a bit as my revelation sinks in. "Good point. How did you learn to be so calculating?"

"My father," I say without even thinking. A fresh wave of gratitude swells within me, hardening my resolve. I can sometimes still feel his presence while battling through all this.

"He must be a great father."

"He was," I reply with a finite tone. That's it. That's all I'll say about that.

I look away and start walking. I have no idea where I'm headed, just somewhere far from here, somewhere I can breathe. I need air. I concentrate on my breathing while my eardrums fills with an almost deafening beat.

Charles steps right behind me. "Hey, it's ok. I'm here for you if you need me." He touches my lower back gently with his rough hands.

My body stills in shock, like it doesn't know how to handle comforting human gestures anymore. *Am I crazy?* I look into his green eyes and the ever-present calmness. He puts me at ease as my shoulders lower and my breathing regulates, all the while his gaze is steady.

His hand glides from my back around to my side, tenderly placed upon my hip. Surprisingly, I don't smack his hand away. "I won't push you to talk about anything you don't want to talk about or to make you do anything you don't want to do, okay?"

I still don't move, only observing his mouth while he talks to me. His lips are smaller in size but move with such force and assurance. I hadn't noticed them before because his scruff covers more than half his face. I find him more and more attractive the longer we converse.

Damn, I'm losing focus.

"Okay," I whisper. It's all I can say.

The glint in his eyes says he doesn't quite believe me yet. "Has anyone told you how beautiful you are?" He brushes a strand of hair away from my face and tucks it behind my ear. He studies my expression, dwelling first on my eyes, then my nose, and my lips.

Did he really just ask me that?

I open my mouth to respond. A rush of unwelcoming answers come to mind, like for him to mind his own business or that it's creepy if that is what is on his mind right now and he should get in line with the guard who strangled me days ago. Or maybe I should just settle for a blunt "yes" and walk away. But I decide to not say anything. Everything right now is just a little too much to handle.

He watches the different emotions roll across my face and chuckles. "I'm glad you decided to take the compliment. I was ready to fight you on it." Charles smiles and continues our walk.

We leave a trail of carvings in the tree bark to mark where we pass. A person can easily get lost in these woods. All the trees look the same, and there are no landmarks to give any sort of clue as to where we are.

As we meander the woods, Charles talks about his family, friends, and rice farm while I quietly listen, leaving my guard up. The more he opens up, though, my walls slowly weaken as the day wears on. Charles has a way about him. He's comforting, funny, and soft spoken yet strong and protective. Whenever we hear a noise, he moves to stand in front of me to face the unknown forest life. Being with him feels easy and just…right.

Coming from the depths of hell, being treated terribly and targeted by demons, and living the same nightmare over and over again, Charles is a light I can't help but be drawn to. Maybe he is my savior and will fill this void of darkness that has entered my soul. We are prisoners in this sick and twisted game. But in another life perhaps, Charles and I could make sense together. I imagine life would be easy with him.

As he tells his stories, I learn that he is a hard worker with a successful business, just like me. I could see us falling in love, not because of what we have or what we would inherit through marriage but just because of…us.

Wow, my thoughts are running wild. I just met the man earlier today.

Unfortunately, we will never know. I at least can be glad for the company of a kind person in an opportunity to reconnect with the outside world.

Around each tree, various berry plants offer a different, albeit temporary, sustenance until we must return to the hole for "dinner." Charles and I also spot some brave rabbits and squirrels that finally emerge from their hiding spots. We plan on catching them over the course of this game for food. We craft sharp spears and other tools for hunting and protection, just in case, from large sticks that we find.

The sun begins to set. The trees cast larger shadows on the ground that tell us it is time to head back. Charles and I bury our weapons under some dirt and leaves and mark the spot so we can find them when we return, whenever that may be. We then approach the clearing where the guards wait for us.

Before we branch off in different directions. Charles grabs my hand. I turn to face him.

"I've had a great time with you today," he confesses, catching me off guard, still, with his touch and heartfelt words.

"I did too," I reply as I break into a full, unexpected smile. My cheeks ache from the long-unpracticed gesture.

Charles returns my smile and leans in slowly. He continues closer, and his eyes drop to my mouth. He faintly touches his lips to mine. My entire body tingles from the delicate kiss. He lingers for a precious moment before he leans back.

"I'll meet you here tomorrow, or whenever they allow us back out here."

He picks up a sharp stick from the ground and carves a heart into one of the tree branches with the initials "G + C" inside. My lips hang open as I watch him walk away.

I touch my mouth, still feeling his soft caress, but I drop my hand when I hear a noise nearby. My body braces, on high alert. How silly that I had forgotten there are other prisoners scouring the forest too. *Did someone just witness us? The guards?*

I don't want to stick around long enough to find out who it is so I run as fast as I can through the forest until I return to the clearing and my imprisonment. As I approach the guards, I see Charles in the distance talking to the asshole who didn't want me as part of his entourage. Several more boys stand close by. He obviously recruited a few others to join his group. Is he still trying to bring Charles into the fold?

My heart beats slow in disappointment. Maybe I am better off alone. Maybe I don't need anyone. Maybe no one needs me either.

CHAPTER 10

I LIE IN MY CELL PONDERING THE EVENTS OF THE DAY, TRYING TO process everything—the long imprisonment, the unexpected chance to go outside, the game, human interaction, human interaction with a good-looking guy, human interaction with a good-looking guy with a great personality who is thoughtful and kind, and oh yeah, the kiss. Oh. My. God. The. Kiss. I'm hopeless. How can I not be. However, seeing him talking to the asshole and the group of boys around him confused me.

My thoughts drift to Charles when I should be assessing my chances for escape. Now that I know we are allowed outside more than once, I need a better plan.

I was right. No one found the flag on the first day. We all returned to the clearing by the hole empty handed. Some prisoners held the look of defeat, especially those who sprinted off like there was no tomorrow. *Well, who the hell knows? Maybe there won't be a tomorrow for us.* Other prisoners seemed refreshed from the outdoors and ready for another day surviving this hell hole.

Again, those green eyes infiltrate my brain and my body. Something awakened in me that hasn't been there before.

Desire.

My body seems to tingle all over, like a rush. I can't wait to see him, and I am happy knowing I will have another opportunity outside again soon. Hopefully tomorrow.

My eyes close, but my mind remains wide awake as these thoughts swirl in my head. I try to quiet the noise by thinking of my father and mother. Maybe they can help me fall asleep.

I imagine myself back in my bed at my house, and everything is normal again. I remember one happy Christmas morning, I ran down the stairs excited to see what Santa brought for me. I opened my first baby doll and wanted to take care of her and bring her around everywhere I went. My mother made breakfast while my father sat next to me underneath the tree. I was content and safe.

My breaths start to slow, and I drift into a pleasant slumber.

A loud noise startles me. My body flies into a sitting position, and I gasp for air.

What was that?

I glance around my lonely cell and notice my bowl arrived. I look at the shit food, take a breath, and decide to swallow it down as fast as I can. It doesn't taste any better than the day before. By now, I thought I would have gotten used to it a little bit. *Hell no.*

But today is different. I feel different.

I know I have to keep my energy up, especially because I may burn calories walking around in the woods. Besides, the unknown of my next meal is a little unnerving. In my time here, I have lost weight—more than I'd like. My slender, athletic build is now just slender and borderline unhealthy. However, my mental state is more important than the physical. Mentally, I have a lot to prove. My life doesn't end here. I still have hope.

The lock on my door disengages, and I instinctively move to the back of the cell. The door seems to take forever to swing open, and I wonder who or what could be on the other side. Finally, the guard who led me outside yesterday stands in the doorway.

Great. His cocky smirk already pisses me off. *What does he want with me?*

He slowly walks toward me, his large frame taking up a lot of room in this small space. I immediately think about how I could charge him and run as fast as I can out of here. I wish I had a utensil to stab him.

Then the rational part of me remembers I have nowhere to go. Who knows the countless number of other guards, servants, maids, and butlers roaming around the grounds. It only takes one to catch me and bring me back down here. Moreover, a hefty punishment would follow after.

My breaths and heart beats quicken with each step he takes.

"You know, you're a pretty little thing, aren't you?"

I shudder. Charles expressing how beautiful I am was way more polished than this. Bile forms in my stomach, and my throat starts to burn. I didn't grab my empty bowl to use as a weapon this time.

Shit.

He inches his way forward. "You want to play a game, sweetheart?" he asks provocatively.

"Don't call me sweetheart, you disgusting bastard!"

"Oh, a little feisty, are you? I knew I saw fire in your eyes yesterday, not just anger from me hitting that stupid boy. But you seem rebellious, untamable, a challenge. It's such a turn on."

He stops about arm's length away. His beady eyes stare at me, trying to bore a hole through my shapeless dress. He looks me up and down while licking his lips. He doesn't touch me, yet. But I notice the bulge in his pants only continues to grow. He really is turned on by my defiance.

Sick bastard.

He watches for my reaction. I consider spitting on him, but I don't want to provoke him into trying to rape me. I must stay calm.

I hold my wrists out for him and say, "I believe you came to retrieve me for the game."

Yes, I want to play a game, not the game he wants to play though. I really hope there is a game upstairs today. Otherwise, he could tie my hands and have his way with me, and I offered myself up to him. *Please, if there is still a God through all this hell, please let there actually be a game today.*

He doesn't move for a long time, each moment making me second guess my actions. Then he pulls the rope from behind his back.

"That's too bad. I was ready for a fight."

He ties my wrists together and leans in closely, too closely. His hands slide around to my lower back, and he presses my whole body against his. I feel how hard he is for me. I would knee him in the ballocks, but his tight grip prohibits me from lifting my legs. His hands lower, grazing over my backside, and he squeezes my buttocks.

Oh my God, what have I done? I can't breathe. I can't abide his behavior.

"I will have you, one way or another. But we don't have time right now."

My knees want to give way with sudden relief, but he grabs my small frame and shoves me out into the tunnel and up the stairs. My body trembles from the shock, and I try not to stumble. As I feel the sun's heat warm my face, I welcome the false sense of freedom.

Outside, all the prisoners line up facing the woods. This time, most of their faces reflect determination. Now we know what to expect a little more than before, not only of the game but also our entire stay thus far.

I see Charles first, and he looks at me with a gentle smile. I want to smile back, but my guard shoves me again.

"Keep moving," he grunts as we walk by more prisoners and guards.

"Prick," I whisper.

"Hey, Theo, ya might wanna tell yer pet to keep 'er mouth shut if she knows what's good for 'er."

Shit.

"Don't worry. I plan on stuffing her mouth with something big later. Then she definitely won't be able to talk. I'll make sure her jaw is nice and sore, maybe even broken."

His words bring on first disbelief and then disgust. I won't let that happen. I'll fight him, and I'll bite him.

I reach the end of the line. My guard, Theo, stands in front of me and unties my wrists. When he releases the rope, he grabs my wrists hard and tugs me to look at him.

"You make me look like a fool again up here, I'll make sure you can't walk or eat for the rest of your stay. You got that?" I remain silent. I can't promise anything. "I said, you got me?" Theo asks louder, forcing my face closer to his.

I look at him with defiant eyes.

He brushes my face with one of his hands. "Oh, I am going to have so much fun with you when you get back."

I push his arm out the way and run as fast as I can. I sprint into the wooded forest, longing for its peace and serenity, away from Theo's nasty thoughts.

By this time, all the other prisoners are released. I try to forget what I'm running away from and shift to what is now ahead of me today. I can't wait to see Charles.

I remember the heart he carved into the tree with our initials. It's etched into my brain as well. I run as fast as I can, not wanting to miss any moment of today with him.

Yesterday, Charles explained that although he looked up to his father his entire life, he was also mistreated by him. His father hit or yelled at him over the smallest mistakes. No wonder Charles is so comforting. He recognizes my insecurities and tries to make me feel safe. He was robbed of such comfort as a child and teenager and by the hands of his own father no less.

I couldn't imagine.

My father was always a voice of reason. He never reacted violently out of spite or to prove he was the authoritative figure. He wanted me to understand why my mistakes were wrong and how to become a better person from them.

I lose sight of the clearing and begin to look for our carvings in the tree trunks. *Damn, there are so many trees!* I feel lost already. I swivel my head from side to side looking for any of our unique clues. Finally, I find a few trees with carvings and follow the path to the heart with our initials.

I slow my pace but find myself alone. *What did I expect?* I guess that means I can't be disappointed. *Right?*

I wait by the tree for a few minutes to give Charles time to find me. Maybe he got lost. Or maybe he doesn't want to partner with me. Maybe, last night in his cell, he realized that I wasn't good enough. That I would only hold him back. I would be the cause of his death, just like my parents.

No. Stop thinking this way.

I need to get on with this. I need to get on with my life, or what is left of it.

I walk to the pile of weapons that Charles and I hid. I grab the short tomahawk I made and a long spear to throw. The other tools that Charles made are still where we left them, which tells me he hasn't been here yet.

Damn, am I really that bad?

Negative thoughts swirl in my head until my stomach cries for attention. I haven't had much to eat these days, and my body is now finally aware of the danger it is in without energy to sustain it. Today, I will hunt for food. There is no flag, not today, not for me. So here I go, on my own, to hunt.

What the hell am I doing?

I channel back to my days in the strawberry fields, helping my father harvest the crops. I take a deep breath in and transform into that tough farm girl, who doesn't take no for an answer.

I hear rustling in the woods to my left. I lower myself behind a tree and wait for whatever animal presents itself. I hope for a bunny as they have great lean meat to keep me going for a while.

The noise continues to stir, and I prepare to make my move. I can almost taste the delicious meat before I even see the living animal. Then, the noise stops. I wait a minute in silence. Still nothing. Should I continue to wait for the perfect opportunity or just end this bunny's life before it runs off?

It's my turn to create my own destiny. I need to eat, or I'll be the one dead.

I slowly stalk my prey, walking as quietly as possible. I see the bright, white tail on the bunny as he nibbles on a nearby leaf. His tail lightly shakes as he feeds himself. Little does he know, this is his last supper. I raise my tomahawk high in the air, ready to give it a full swing. Goodbye, sweet bunny. I lower my arm as swiftly as I can, but the bunny bolts. He startles, as am I, when male laughter comes from my right.

Damn it!

I hide, annoyed, behind the tree as a group of boys talk to one another. I can't believe my meal was interrupted by such lame, ignorant pubescents.

"You should have seen the look on your face!" One of the boys asks another. This pitch of his voice is higher, like he is just on the brink of puberty.

Figures.

"The look on my face? What about Charles's face?" another one responds with a bit of a lower tone. He must be older.

Charles? So he did leave me. Alone.

I feel like an idiot for trusting someone, like a slap in the face. Well at least now I know before we became more—more hurt, more lies, more emptiness. I feel hollow.

Now what do I do? Do I sit here, listen, and continue to hide, or do I jump out and attack these fuckers?

"Shut up!" Charles suddenly yells.

"Aww, did someone hurt your feelings, Charles?" the higher pitched voice goads. "Or what about your girlfriend we saw you kissing yesterday?"

"I said, shut up!" Charles shouts louder. I hear bodies wrestling on the ground amid punching and grunting. But I can't tell who is winning. Honestly, at this point, I really don't care. Well, only a little. I thought Charles liked me.

"Fight! Fight! Fight!" a few of them chant together.

I hear more groaning and rustling around. Their footsteps seem to be getting closer to me.

"Oomph!" says an unknown voice.

"Look at him squirm. He can't even throw a decent punch," one asshole says.

Then it stops—the wrestling, the noises, the voices. All goes silent except for someone's heavy breathing.

"Too bad Charles can't handle the guards talking about his girlfriend. And too bad you can't do anything to them anyway. They will kill you," the lower voice threatens.

"Not if I kill them first. And you!" Charles rebuts.

"Let's leave him. He's no good to us anyway. He's a wimp. Look at him. He's already huffing and puffing after one fight."

"It's three against one, you assholes!" Charles proclaims.

A sense of guilt overwhelms me. I don't know what happened, but perhaps it wasn't all his fault for leaving me alone this morning. I wait for the others to leave.

Their voices fade in the distance. I think the coast is clear to finally peak around the tree. Charles sits on the ground, propped against another tree, with his shoulders slumped in defeated. His bottom lip is cut, and his shirt has blood smears, likely from him wiping his face.

As I approach him, his face lifts. A flash of fear shines in his eyes that quickly turns into surprise and then sadness. The closer I get, I see that one of his eyes is starting to swell shut. Three against one isn't fair, but I thought he would have had more injuries.

He doesn't say anything as I crouch next to him. I can't decide if I am still mad at him or not. Regardless, he looks worn out, and I need to help him.

"Are you hurt?" I kneel down and evaluate his lip and eye.

He hisses in pain as I touch his face before replying, "No, not too bad. I'll be all right."

"Where were you this morning?" I abruptly ask, desperation infecting my tone. Charles turns his head away, and I can't look at him either. I look away. I feel rejected. Silence. "Forget I asked."

"No! That's not it," Charles states, turning back toward me quickly.

I sit there, waiting, still looking off into the distance. I feel like a fool, my emotions all over the place—I like him, I'm mad at him, and I'm confused by him.

"I couldn't meet you this morning."

"Why?"

"Those guys were watching you. They made comments."

"What comments?"

"I'm not going to tell you. They aren't ones any lady should hear."

"A guard made them too?"

"How did you know that?" His eyes widen in surprise and he grimaces again in pain.

"I heard those jerks talking about it, and then a fight broke out. I don't know who said what, but I heard you get upset."

"Well, I'm glad you stayed hidden because they would have more than likely tried to capture you and do who knows what."

My stomach clenches in fear. I'd like to think I'd kick their asses, but even Charles had a hard time. He was outnumbered. I would have been too.

"Stay away from everyone, if possible," Charles says as he tries to stand. He groans and holds a hand over his ribs, the other resting against the tree to hold himself upright.

"Here, let me help." I struggle to support him on his feet.

It's impossible to stay away from everyone when it is mandatory for all of us to report back at the end of each day. The words of Theo warning me about my return to his care resonate in my mind. I will do anything to stay away from him as long as possible.

"I know you're hurt but are you able to walk around today?" I ask Charles as he looks like he is struggling to breathe. He stands against the tree trunk.

"Yeah, sure," he states painfully. He turns around carefully.

Even with his torn, bloody clothes, busted lip, and black eye, he still looks undeniably handsome.

I glance down at my dirty gown. My current state of filth makes me question how he could ever find me attractive.

When I look up, I find Charles staring at me. My eyes lock onto his. How long has he been witnessing my self-evaluation?

I'm horrified. He lets out a chuckle.

"What's so funny?" I timidly ask.

"You."

I do not know how to respond. My emotions are sensitive from being left alone this morning, to moments ago hearing Charles get beat up by fellow prisoners, to now feeling unwanted and unclean. *What is happening here?*

"Don't do that," Charles states.

"Do what?"

"Doubt yourself."

"How do you know—"

"Because you have a confidence about you that no one else has." He takes a few steps toward me. "You constantly have a fire in your eyes that is ready to burn anything in its way." He gently touches my shoulder. "Don't allow anyone or anything to make you forget why you are here and what you need to do. Even yourself. Ok?"

Well, when you put it that way.

"Ok."

"Let's go."

Charles and I walk silently for a bit. The sun is high in the trees. Its rays cast down in slivers between the leaves. Warmth touches my face every time I stand in its light. Beads of sweat form on my forehead, and I try to wipe them away. But they keep persisting just like the heavy, humid air. Breathing becomes more of a chore in the dense forest. There's nowhere for the water vapor to escape. It's trapped, just like my life at the current moment.

I look over at Charles, and he seems to be having a hard time as well. His heavy breathing causes him to grab his rib cage as he tries to comfort his pain. He winces as he slowly reaches up his arm to wipe the sweat off his discolored face. His right wrist is held closely to his chest as he massages it with his left hand. He walks with a slight limp while we wander into the unknown.

Until this point, my life had a path. My mother and father would say it was to be wed and have children. I would say it was to sustain the family strawberry business. Either path contained hope and freedom. Now, here I am, a prisoner, wandering between trees that all look the same, not having a clue on what direction we head in. My surroundings are the same each day, yet, all of this is so unpredictable. Nothing is making sense. Life seems meaningless.

"Hey, what is that?"

Charles points to something in the distance. With a black eye, I'm surprised he can still see well. My eyesight has always been sharp, but lately with my lack of sleep, sometimes it's hard to tell what's right in front of me. I squint to see what he found.

An object sticks up from the ground with bright, colorful… flowers?

"I don't know."

I have an eerie feeling.

"Let's get closer," Charles says as he starts to pick up his pace.

I'm just as curious as Charles, but I'm more cautious. Why would a random patch of colorful flowers be in the middle of this dark forest? And how?

We approach the object and stand in silence.

"Who is H. Sullivan?" Charles kneels by the tombstone and brushes dirt off the worn stone to find more information.

"I don't know."

"Well, there doesn't appear to be any phrase on it, nor can I find any dates. It has either come off with time or it wasn't on there to begin with. This must be old."

"If it's that old, why are their fresh flowers here?"

I'm perplexed at the beautiful arrangement of flowers—white camellias, purple azaleas, red and yellow snapdragons, and my favorite Louisiana irises: Black Gamecocks. I'm equally disturbed how the fresh cut, colorful arrangement settled next to the neglected, grotesque headstone.

I look around the gravesite to see if I can find tracks of any kind. But there are none.

"Well, whoever this is, I can't decide if he or she was loved or despised," Charles states plainly as he stands upright.

"I agree. Someone had to have been here recently. These flowers are fresh. Yet, the stone appears abandoned."

"I can't tell where we are. We must be close to something if outside people are coming in."

"I haven't seen these types of flowers in these woods, so I think you're right. Someone is bringing them in from a different location. But from where?"

I look around, but all the trees look the same. We haven't been marking the trees to trace our tracks like we did yesterday. How would we know how to get back here or out of here?

"We should start to head back. I think we may be really lost," I say to Charles.

I don't want to head back, but in case I'm right and this takes longer than expected, I don't want to get an unnecessary beating.

Charles looks around. "What direction shall we take?"

I close my eyes, spin around, and point off in the distance.

"Let's go… this way."

I open my eyes to see where we will start our journey.

Charles laughs. "I think we should head this way." He points in the complete opposite direction.

"Was I off that much?"

"Well, if my sense of direction is correct, my path will be closer to the way we came here and maybe where I started from this morning."

This morning. It seems so long ago. But yes, I remember. I was left alone. I'm glad I'm not alone any longer.

"Ok, let's see where you are taking us."

"Don't be such a smartass."

Now, it is my turn to laugh at Charles. I haven't had someone poke fun with me in a long time. My face and heart feel good with the unfamiliar emotion.

We make our way slowly back to the clearing. We forgo the animals in the forest today. We do not have the energy to catch one. Instead, we pick some berries for our slim dinner. Charles looks at me when we approach trees with our markings on them from yesterday. He smiles—his boyish grin, a true and genuine comfort. His sense of direction was right.

Relief fills my body.

"You did it! You got us back on track." I give Charles a big hug. I wrap my arms around his body and squeeze with my excited emotions. He winces a little in pain.

"Oh! Sorry."

"No, it's ok. My ribs are still tender from this morning."

I put my hands gently on his ribs. I feel bad the other prisoners did that to him, and it was partly my fault. He was defending me.

He takes my hands. "It's ok. I'm fine."

I look up into his eyes. His green, tender eyes look right back at me.

I close my eyes and begin to lean in toward Charles's lips. I can't control my body. Everything about him makes it so easy for me to like. I don't know if he feels the same way, but right now, I really don't care.

I feel the heat from his face. I know he is just inches away from touching me, but I don't want to seem desperate. So I wait for him to make the final move.

At that moment, I feel an unwanted sting on my ankle and heat rising up my leg.

"Ooowwww!" I yell out in pain as I fall to the ground and grab my right ankle.

I see Charles looking down at me with baffled eyes. "Are you ok?"

I hear noises right around my feet. Sticks and leaves shift around on the ground, but I can't tell what lies amongst them. My ankle and leg radiate pain, and I am unable to stand upright. Tears form in the corners of my eyes as the pain takes over my body.

"Oh my God," Charles claims.

"W…what is it?"

"Grace, I need to get you to a doctor, now!"

The urgency of his voice isn't helping my physical and mental state. "What was it, Charles?"

"It's a snake. I think a cottonmouth snake. Grace, hold on."

Charles swoops me up into his arms and begins to run. I crouch my head into his chest as tears begin to flow. I don't know much about snakes, but from Charles's reaction, this cannot be good. I try to stay still as he holds onto me tightly and runs with all the energy he has left in his body. From today's earlier events, I don't know how he has anything left.

My right ankle throbs, and sharp pains shoot up my leg. My heart races faster and my breaths become short.

We make it to the clearing, and Charles starts to yell, "Help! Help!" He runs up to the first guard he sees.

"Please, help her. I beg you!"

"What happen'd to her?" a familiar, unpleasant voice asks Charles.

"A snake bite. A venomous one. Please, help me!"

"I think you're mistaken boy. We don't care to help anyone here."

"I'll do anything. Please, help her." Charles voice starts to shake. It sounds like he's on the verge of tears.

My body begins to go numb, but I twist my head with the little energy I have left to see Theo's face before I give up.

The look of surprise on his face catches me off guard right as I close my eyes.

"Whatta ya need me to do, boy?"

"We need something sharp to cut her open and drain the venom," Charles quickly states before I fall into darkness.

CHAPTER
11

MY HEAD HURTS.

My right ankle hurts worse.

My whole body is supine on a cold floor. I try to move a little, but everything inside of me tells me to stay put.

I can't. I need to find Charles. *Where is he? And what happened to me?*

"Don't move chil'."

I hear Hanna's voice, but I can't see her.

"Hanna?"

"Yessum."

"Where am I?"

"Yo in da room where we first met."

I look around a bit more and notice a chair with bloody cloths that lay all over it. I also notice a table with bread and fruit. My mouth begins to salivate.

"Dat food is fo you chil', but you cannot have dem yet. You will throw dat up if you have dem now. Yo still need to wait another day before you can have it."

"Another day?! How long have I been in here?"

"Yo been in here two days. I've been told by Theo to take good care of ya. Not sho why but I'm glad that he wants yo betta."

I shudder at the thought of Theo. His hot breath and gross teeth are enough to make me want to throw up the food that's on the table before I even eat it.

"My head hurts. Can I please have some water?"

"Yessum."

Hanna fetches me a glass of water, and I drain the contents quickly. I look down at my ankle and notice that Hanna has been doing a great job of tending to my injury and keeping me alive.

This short conversation has me exhausted. All I can do is close my eyes and allow Hanna to continue her progress. I fall back into a state of slumber, knowing that I'll be able to see Charles again soon.

The next day, I make a full recovery and eat all the food provided to me. I feel revitalized and have my energy back.

There is a knock at the door, and Hanna goes to open it.

Theo stands in the doorway.

Ugh.

"Hello, Grace." Theo stares at me with hungry eyes.

I don't respond.

"Time to go."

"Where are we going?" I don't know what this man plans to do with me. I don't trust him.

"Back to the game. Everyone misses you."

Charles!

I stand up but stumble over myself. It's been a few days since I've stood upright. This simple task now feels foreign.

"She needs mo' time," Hanna states.

"No, she doesn't. She's ready. The others are dropping off, and we need her back out there. I don't need anyone in the house getting suspicious."

Huh?

I take a few steps and begin to balance better. It doesn't take long before I follow Theo out of the doorway. I turn back around and look at Hanna. "Thank you."

"Yo welcome chil'."

I cross the threshold, and Theo immediately grabs my arm.

"You owe me one," he says with his putrid breath in my ear.

"I don't owe you shit."

He spins me around to face him. Before I realize what is happening, he grabs my back and presses me against his body. He gropes by backside and licks the side of my neck. Then he takes a big whiff of my scent by my ear.

"I said you owe me one. And you will. I will have you how I please. If it wasn't for me, you'd be dead."

I know in my heart that it was Charles who saved me. Not Theo.

I headbutt Theo and elbow him in the throat. I know I shouldn't have done that, but I have to get away from him as far as I can. I don't want him to take advantage of me. Theo is overweight. There is a slim chance he could catch me, but I won't let him. I don't have any rope or chains weighing me down, but I am weak. I try to sprint as fast as I can toward the forest.

My ankle is sore, but I'm in better shape than what I was in before I was bitten. A little food goes a long way. I'm back into the wild and ready to take on whatever happens next. I hold a newfound strength, and I can't wait to see Charles. I run to our meeting spot in hopes that he will be there.

I have a hard time navigating where I am. I try to think back to when I first arrived at the plantation and when I first entered the forest. I look back and don't see Theo anywhere. I'm glad that fat ass can't catch up to me.

I slow down to catch my breath and follow my instincts to locate the tree with the carved heart.

Not much time passes before I see the man I'm looking for standing next to it.

Time itself seems to slow down. His face breaks into a big smile, and my own mirrors him. My tired legs find the energy to jump in his arms, and I hug him tightly.

He laughs out loud, the vibrations echoing through my own chest. I pull back to look at his handsome face and slowly lean in to kiss him. Such sparks from a soft kiss. He rests his forehead against mine, and our heavy breaths mingle between us.

"Well, hello there, Grace."

"Hi," I greet him out of breath.

He chuckles and sets my feet back on the ground.

"You're here. I can't believe it." Charles looks at me like I am a rare commodity.

"Yep! A snake bite can't get rid of me that easily."

"Grace, a cottonmouth snake isn't just any old snake. I was really worried about you."

"I know you were. It frightened me to see how scared you were."

"Well, how do you feel?"

"Honestly, I feel fine. I slept for two days straight. I ate some bread and hydrated before coming out here. My ankle is a little sore, but I don't have much to complain about. How about you? What have I missed?"

We collect our buried weapons, and he holds my hand as we walk and talk. We continue our journey, breaching farther into the unknown woods.

"I've been a nervous wreck," Charles bluntly states.

"Oh."

"Yeah. I haven't eaten or slept much because I can't stop thinking about you. I thought you may be dead."

"I'm sorry to make you worry."

"Don't be silly. It's not your fault. No one told me anything. I tried to ask, but every time I opened my mouth I got slapped with no verbal response. I came out to our tree and waited. I figured when you were well, you would know to meet me here. Which you did."

I look over at Charles's face and catch a peak at his dimpled cheek before he sheepishly looks away. He squeezes my hand a little. Swiftly, he lifts me up and spins me around with an enormous smile on his face. I laugh out loud as he places me back down beside him, and we continue our walk without missing a beat.

"So you stayed by our tree all day waiting for me?"

"Not all day. I told myself that I would wait for the sunlight to rise up through the trees. As the first rays hit my face, it was time for me to continue so when you would return, we'd have a more distinct path to search."

"Did you discover anything?"

"No."

"Oh. Well, which way should we go?"

"I don't know. The last few days didn't lead anywhere."

"Oh well, at least you tried." I chuckle.

"I guess. I felt worthless. Without you, it was quite boring meandering about by myself."

"So no one has found the flag?"

"Nope."

"Hmm. Something just isn't right. I want this nightmare to end. It's frustrating not knowing the end game. They said we have a purpose. But what? Why are we all here?"

Our previous playfulness shifts to a more serious dedication to solving our predicament. Charles's jaw clenches. I had never seen such a hard countenance on him before. His whole posture stiffens.

"I don't know. But whoever is behind this is going to pay. I'll make sure of it. I want to see them in the grave." I believe him. And I want a piece of the action.

"Count me in. If I could do the honors, I will." All of the horrid moments since I arrived here replay through my mind.

He snaps his head toward me. My ambition for revenge shocks him. We agree on one thing for sure. We aren't going down without a fight.

"Do you think you can live with taking a man's life?"

"I couldn't live with myself if I didn't try. I have been beaten and almost raped several times by Theo. So, no, I wouldn't regret it if the chance presented itself."

As he absorbs my confession, I watch as his expression contorts with rage, like a caged beast about to unleash all its flesh on an unfortunate prey. His mouth snaps shut, and he balls his fists. He works to control his breathing as he counts to ten with his eyes closed.

I try to reassure him. "I'm fine, as you can see."

He opens his green eyes and looks straight into my blue ones. "You're *fine*?! You're anything but fine! This whole place isn't fine! This whole situation is all fucked up. On top of that, they beat you and almost rape you? You been bitten by a poisonous snake, and you still come out here, hold your head high, and act like nothing is wrong?"

His eyes soften around the edges as his rage for them turns to compassion for me. He runs his fingers down my arm.

"I've never met anyone as smart or brave as you. How do you find the strength to keep going?"

The words clog in my throat. I stare forward into the nothingness, seeing fields of strawberries instead of this forest. "For my parents. I don't want their deaths to be in vain. I need to survive this place and kill the men who murdered my mother and father."

I sit on a nearby broken tree trunk. Charles is still speechless. I decide to finally share about that night. Maybe he will understand and stop looking at me like I'm a porcelain doll. I take a deep breath.

"Two men came into my plantation house in the middle of the night, uninvited. They busted through the windows and killed both my parents at gun point. I tried to escape out my bedroom window, but I didn't get there in time. They also brought me here by horse coach, just like you. Every time I try to find an opportunity to escape, I start to think rationally. They have too many people who monitor the grounds. I don't even know where we are, in what town or state. Even if I was lucky enough to break out, I would eventually be found and probably tortured and killed. I can't let that happen. My parents made the ultimate sacrifice for me. I have to survive for them."

Charles leans in and kisses me, longer, deeper. My stomach flutters with desire.

He whispers, "I want to help you. I want to take all your pain away. Please let me take care of you any way I can."

"I'm not used to having anyone take care of me."

"Good. Then you don't have anyone to compare it to." He chuckles. I can't help but laugh myself. He makes me happy.

All these years, I convinced myself that I didn't need a man to take care of me. I am a strong woman. My father taught me to be independent. I also didn't know if I would find a man to love me for me or one who simply wanted to inherit the family strawberry business.

Now, I understand what my parents had, how they felt for one another. Yet these developing feelings are still foreign.

"I want you to know that you are not alone anymore. We come as a package deal. None of this 'I can do everything on my own' bullshit. Got it?" Charles stares at me while making his comments.

I reflect on his commitment. I appreciate that he wants to help me, for whatever reasons he feels he has to. Although I don't want any pity help, we probably can accomplish our goals faster as a team. "Fine."

He assesses me for a moment—judging my sincerity and my hesitation. I'm sure most other women would love the opportunity for a man to take care of them. I, however, have been too independent for too long. I view this as an opening for a new partnership and I decide to switch my tone. "Thank you."

Charles quickly responds, "You're welcome. And it will always be my pleasure and my honor to help you any way that I can. So you will just have to deal with it." He winks, and that youthful charm warms my heart. His playfulness wins out, though, and I'm left to do exactly what he says. I just deal with it.

A few hours pass by as we explore and mark trees. We must make some progress because we aren't walking around in circles. Charles and I are thankful for the remaining leaves on these trees for shade in the humid heat. As autumn approaches, leaves continue to fall each day.

Charles abruptly stops and throws his arm toward me. My body slams into his arm as I realize he halted. "What is it?" I ask.

He holds his pointer finger to his lips. We stand still and listen, and after several minutes, I grow restless and uncomfortable in this awkward curiosity. Before I can formulate more questions, a sharp object sails across my face and plunges into the trunk of a nearby tree.

Holy shit, what was that?

Charles grabs my hand, and we take off running as he leads me through the woods. His pace is hard for me to keep up with, and I quickly become short of breath. I release my grip and hunch over, with my hands on my knees.

"Are you hurt?" he asks as he spins back in my direction.

"No, I don't think so." God, I feel so weak. "What was that?"

"Not *what* was that. *Who* was that?"

For the last couple of days, we haven't seen anyone else. I keep forgetting that we aren't alone. "Do you think someone is trying to hurt us?"

"Yes."

"Why?"

"I don't know. Maybe someone sees us as a threat. You saw where that arrow landed on the trunk?"

"It would have pierced my neck." I grab the side of my throat.

"We need to keep moving. Whoever it is may still be after us."

We move more quickly, still marking trees but skipping more in between. Charles and I slowly relax as we believe that time and distance falls between us and the person with the arrows.

"I wonder how many prisoners return before the sun sets tonight," I say, curious who is still alive out here.

"Yeah, I mean if someone really is trying to kill us, who knows how many others they successfully pursued," he speculates as he picks up a rock and throws it up in the air. I notice that he likes to keep his hands busy in times of uncertainty.

Not satisfied with his distraction, he finds a big stick. He tosses his rock once more, this time hitting it with the stick as it falls back toward the ground. We watch it fly through the air

Ping!

The rock bounces off a white stone surface set just off the ground in the distance. Charles and I turn to face each other. *What is that?*

The white stone structure seems out of place in these dark woods. We slowly approach what we realize is a circle.

"A well?" I place my hands on one of the stones.

"What the hell?" Charles mimics my confusion.

I back away and begin searching the ground.

"What are you doing?"

"You'll see." I find a medium-sized rock and hold it in my hand, hovering over the well's opening.

"Are you making a wish?" Charles chuckles to himself.

I chastise him with scornful eyes before turning back to the black hole before me and toss the rock into the well. I count…one…two… *ping!*

"There wasn't a splash," Charles remarks.

"It's not terribly far down either."

"What do you think is down there?"

"I don't know, but I want to find out." I throw one leg onto the stone structure and begin to climb over the top.

"No, stop!" He rushes to my side. "It's getting late." I open my mouth to argue when he puts his fingers over my lips. "I'm just as curious as you are to discover what is or isn't there. But we don't have time. Once one of us climbs down there, who knows how long it will take to climb back out, if we even can."

He has a point.

"We have to make it back to the hole before the sun goes down. This is the farthest we have ever come, and I don't want either of us, especially you, to get in trouble if we don't make it back in time. You have endured too much here already in this god-awful place."

Why does he have to play the gentleman card now?

I start to back away from the well. Charles gathers our weapons when suddenly someone grabs me from behind. I yelp with surprise, causing Charles to turn around.

The man, with big hands and strong grip, holds a sharp blade to my neck. If I try to struggle even the slightest, the sharp object will puncture my throat.

"Don't move a muscle, or the girl dies!" His hot breath against my ear makes me queasy.

"Don't hurt her," Charles pleads. I read his eyes as he assesses the situation. I still don't know who this bastard is. It doesn't sound like Will, Larsen, or Theo.

Then who the hell is it?

My new captor doesn't back down, so Charles continues, "You are just like us. We are only trying to survive. We can all do this together. There is no point in hurting her. You will only make matters worse if you do anything stupid." He speaks in slow, short sentences, not to confuse or startle the man with the weapon.

Another prisoner?

"Don't tell me what to do! The less of you, the more chance for me to find the flag."

Charles looks me in the eyes and asks, "Do you trust me?"

His question distracts me. "What?" I cautiously reply, careful of the sharp object against my throat.

"Do you trust me?"

"Yes." I quickly answer this time because, undoubtedly, I do.

Charles charges us at full speed. I shut my eyes, embracing for impact. I feel the sharp object loosen from my neck so I throw my hand at his arm holding the weapon, creating more distance between me and the blade.

Then, Charles smashes into me like a brick wall, and all three of us collide onto the ground.

Instantly, the two men begin fighting, with me in the middle. Charles punches the prisoner, who cannot move with our two bodies on top of him.

The prisoner attempts to stab Charles. I'm afraid that if I try to squirm out of this brawl, I may cause more damage. Charles clearly has the upper hand.

"Aaarrrghh!" I scream as a sharp pain runs down my side. Charles stiffens on top of me and throws the next punch with a little more rage. He shifts to pin down the prisoner's hand holding the weapon.

I wiggle, as best I can, out of the sandwich battle and scurry away to a nearby tree. I sit down with my back against the tree to assess my wounds. I notice a long scrape down my side that drew blood, but luckily, it doesn't look too deep.

I turn back to the men and see Charles unleash the beast I know is inside of him. It should probably scare me, but it doesn't. The stupid prisoner didn't even have a chance.

Charles hits his face so hard that blood spews everywhere. The man becomes unrecognizable. Finally, his lifeless body stops moving. Charles breathes heavily, glaring at his dead opponent, before turning to search for me.

When he spots me, he climbs off the body, quickly walks toward me, and squats to my level.

"I'm fine," I say before he can ask.

"You are anything but fine," he replies again. "Let me see. Where are you hurt?"

My already soiled dress now sports slashes in the fabric and red marks of blood. "You don't need to see it. I told you I'll be all right."

"Goddamn it! Will you just show me? I have to see for myself!" I know he's only trying to help. He takes a deep breath. I watch him morph his anger into sadness. He continues more calmly, "I won't forgive myself if I caused you any more pain. Please show me."

I slowly lift my dress past my underwear and expose my side and the large wound. The pain radiates from his eyes as he examines the slash. He reaches out to touch my side but hesitates, realizing he has another man's blood on his hands.

"It's really not that bad. I'll be okay."

He hangs his head for a moment and chuckles. "You really are something else, you know that?"

"How so?"

"I wish I could show you. But we don't have much time, and I don't know who else is around here. We should get back to the clearing."

"Well, can I settle for a kiss?"

He doesn't hesitate this time. He takes my lips fiercely and grabs at the back of my head, pulling at my hair. I don't even care that his hands have blood on them. I'm too wrapped up in this moment of desire. I want him.

I grip the sides of his face, deepening our passionate embrace. He reaches for my waist, but I hiss in pain, breaking the kiss.

"I'm sorry," Charles stumbles back. "I didn't mean to hurt you."

"Can you stop apologizing for something you didn't do."

"Ok." He's a roiling ball of anger, passion, and regret. We stare at each other, trying to understand one another.

He stands and holds his hand out for me. I take it, and he helps me stand. Then, we make our way back to the clearing.

<h1 style="text-align: center;">CHAPTER
12</h1>

IT IS A LONG JOURNEY BACK, ESPECIALLY WITH A FEW MORE BREAKS to keep my side from bleeding. We finish marking the trees that were disregarded from the unexpected sprint after the surprise tormentor earlier in the day. But we make it just in time.

Before the guards can spot us coming back together, we stop at our spot with the heart carved in the tree, and Charles turns me to face him. Just like the evening before, he gives me a soft, affectionate kiss.

My mind is in the clouds.

He pulls away after a few minutes and touches his forehead with mine. "I can't wait to see you again tomorrow."

"Me too. Hopefully it will be a better, less eventful day."

"I agree. But any day with you is a great day." He smiles my favorite smile.

I smile back.

"Let's meet here at our spot again. Tomorrow, we will head straight to the well and figure out what is down there."

"Sounds good to me."

He gives me one more quick kiss and slowly backs away. "See you soon, my love."

My breath catches. I can't believe he just called me that. It's too soon, right? I absolutely love it, though.

He laughs at my stunned expression. Then he turns and jogs off into the woods, protecting us from being seen together.

When I finally gather my thoughts, I make my way to the clearing. The guards wait for the surviving prisoners.

My repugnant guard sees me. "Ah, there you are. I see you've survived another day." He's so vile I don't even want to look at him.

He glances down at my side. "Look what we have here." He reaches out to touch my battle wounds. I instinctively swat his hand away, but he catches my hand and tugs me hard, pulling me close to his body. "Still got some fight in you left, I see. I can't wait to see how you kick and scream when I shove my cock in your pretty little cunt."

I spit in his face.

Theo stills, and I witness the shock in his face. He gathers himself and wipes his face with his sleeve. "You bitch!" He slaps me, and my head whips around as I fall to the ground. My whole face radiates with pain, and the pounding is almost unbearable.

Then I hear a familiar voice. "You bastard! Don't touch her!"

Charles.

He runs toward Theo with murder in his eyes. As soon as Charles throws the first punch, I try to yell out, "Stop!" But it comes out in a whisper. Then, my world goes black.

I wake up in my cell, not remembering how I got here. I don't even know if a whole day went by or just a few hours.

All at once, those last moments flood back into my head. My head still hurts from when Theo hit me and from the recent memories.

Charles.

Oh god. What happened to him? Is he okay? Is he still alive? I hope the guards didn't beat him to a pulp. Actually, I hope Charles beat that bastard into bloody shards. I really hope he killed him too. I'm sure multiple guards had to pry Charles off.

Does he know I'm still alive? I fainted right before his eyes. For all he knows, he probably thinks I'm dead.

I hear my door unlock, and a familiar woman appears with items in her hand. "Hanna?" Hanna walks in without looking at me.

"Yo back again so quick?"

She places the objects on the floor and then walks over to me.

"Hanna, what is going on?"

"I dunno, chil'. Dey call me to come down 'ere wit' fresh clothes and bandages. Dey led me to ya do'. And 'ere I is."

She starts to undress me. *Thank god.* She cleans and wraps my wound. The bleeding stopped long ago, but I won't argue because she once again shows me an ounce of kindness in this nasty place.

After I dress in fresh clothes and underwear, Hanna pulls something out of her hidden pocket. She unwraps the item carefully and hands it to me. "I figga who eva the po' soul was I was comma help prob'ly needs some food."

She offers a whole loaf of bread, just for me. I can't help but to scarf down the delicious food. I should cherish what she gave me and take my time, but I didn't realize how famished I was until actual good food is right in front of me.

"Thank you." I look her in the eyes and see a deeper pain hidden there. "Can you help me escape?"

"Chil', I canna do dat."

"Please, help me get out of here. They are torturing us. They feed us shit and make us take shits in our own shitty space. Why won't you help? I know you want to."

"Cuz ya an' I will both get caught. When that happens, we die. I don' wanna die."

I'm getting nowhere. She wants to help, I can tell, but she refuses to follow her heart. "One day, I'll get out of here. I'll figure out a way. So you can either help me or not."

She doesn't say a word, taking in my determination, my will to live. "Good luck, chil'." She starts to walk toward the door.

"By any chance, have you helped out a man too?"

"Da crazy boy who hit those guards? No I have not. Dey carried him off somewhere. I suppose he's dead by now."

My heart sinks. Charles is strong, but he's no match for four or five guards. Once again, I cry myself to sleep.

The next morning, my door opens. I hold my breath, hoping it's not Theo. I don't have any fight left in me. I might just let him take me so he can get it over with.

Instead, another guard stands in the doorway with the rope already out for him to tie my hands.

"Where's Theo?"

"He's immobile at the moment. If you'd like, I can tell him you asked about him. I'm sure he'd like that. I know he is very fond of you."

"No, thank you." I smile at the thought of Theo's bruised face and inability to maneuver around.

The new guard ties my hands and leads me upstairs to the outside world once again. I plan to reunite with Charles by the meeting spot. Hanna said Charles was taken away. Hopefully he has recovered and is able to return to the game.

When all of the prisoners line up, only some of us remain. *What the hell?* I don't see Charles either. Where is he? My heart starts to race. Before I can analyze the situation any further, my hands are untied, and I'm shoved toward the woods.

The other prisoners all disappear into the woods like nothing strange is happening—just another day. I take off running to our meeting spot in hopes of seeing Charles.

I reach the meeting spot and wait. Hopefully, he will meet me here soon. My mind wonders at what could keep him. Maybe the guards detained him for some reason. Who knows what they've done with him after yesterday.

All sorts of scenarios run through my mind, and I can't keep my thoughts straight. Why are there so few of us out here today? Charles did kill a man. And now he has also disappeared. Did the other prisoner actually kill others? *Jesus.*

I know Charles would be mad at me if I just sat here like a lost puppy and waited for him. He would want me to start without him. The daylight is precious.

I feel the first rays of light hit my face and decide to leave. I retrieve one of my sharp sticks in case I need to defend myself again and run in the direction of the well.

CHAPTER 13

I MAKE IT TO THE WELL UNHARMED. I STOPPED A FEW TIMES TO CATCH my breath, not remembering how far away it was, but I kept my breaks short in case someone followed me.

I set my weapon on the ground, ignoring the dead body still nearby, and look into the well. It is dark, but I know it isn't very deep.

How do I get down there by myself?

I had hoped Charles would have a plan for this part. I look around for some magical rope to just suddenly appear out of thin air. Unfortunately, this isn't an enchanted forest. I find absolutely nothing, except leaves, sticks, and rocks.

Please, God, give me strength.

The well is not very wide, and the stones are not evenly spaced. I will use my legs to guide me down by placing them on either sides of the well walls, and my hands can grip individual stones for support in case I slip. I grab a small rock and place it in my mouth so I can check my distance from the bottom as I maneuver down the well.

Please don't fall. Please don't fall.

I inch my way down very slowly. After just a couple of minutes, beads of sweat form along my forehead, and my legs start to shake. My strength is not like it used to be a couple of weeks ago.

Thinking of all of the hard times I have endured since being captured motivates me to keep going. I think about my parents, Will, Larsen, Theo, the gash in my side, and everything in between. I continue to move down as my body becomes numb. I welcome the blanket feeling. Downward I go. Down. Down.

Man, this is harder and farther than I thought. My right foot slips from a broken brick. *Shit!*

I lose my concentration but catch myself. I almost swallow the rock in mouth from my sudden gasp. I spit out the rock to not only check my distance but so I don't choke and die in this god-forsaken abandoned well.

Quickly, I hear the *ping!* Yes! I'm almost there.

I think of Charles. I embrace the warmth that he brings to my soul. He awakens my senses that I trained to bury deep inside to survive. I decide I want to feel again, for Charles. I take a deep breath, and the stuffy, dusty aroma of the well enters my nostrils, mouth, and lungs.

I close my eyes and let go. I tuck my legs underneath me and fall the rest of the way down. I land with a thud. Very ungracefully. And hard.

Ouch!

I look up and see the light coming out of the top of the well. *I made it!*

"Charles, I hope you find me down here," I quietly talk to myself. I hope he's okay. I hope I'm ok. I stand up and assess myself. I'm a little sore but not bad enough to stop me.

I investigate my new surroundings and wonder why there is no water here. I graze my hands along the walls of the pitch black well. I feel the stones, clay, and dirt that once again dirty my porcelain hands. Then, all of a sudden, the wall disappears, and I face plant onto the cold ground beneath me.

God, that hurt!

I stand up, but hit my head on something hard. "Ouch!" I raise my arms to rub my head, but my hand hits the ceiling above me. Are the walls closing in?

I'm in some sort of tunnel. *Where does this lead to?* My heartrate quickens, reminding me of the close quarters of my cell, and I feel an urgency to get out of here. I wave my hands in front of me to make sure I don't walk into another wall, and every now and then, I continue to touch the ceiling to see if the elevation changes.

I walk aimlessly in the dark for a while before I glimpse a light ahead. I pick up my pace with some kind of end in sight. However, the closer I approach the light, it adopts a peculiar appearance. It remains only a sliver of light coming from above a narrow set of stairs.

Is this a trap? I start to question myself. I don't know where the hell I am. Should I go back and wait for Charles? But deep down inside, I know I can't go back. I'm too far into this. And how do I climb back out the well, anyway?

I take a deep breath and climb the stairs. A small wooden hatch hovers parallel to the last few steps over my head. This is where the light is coming out of. *My exit out of here!* I listen for any sounds on the other side of this wooden hatch. When I don't hear anything, I figure the coast is clear.

Please open.

My heart beats fast as I push gently at first. The hatch starts to open! I climb out of the tunnel.

What the hell?

I spin around in a room in a small cottage, like the one they brought me to when I first met Hanna. A long table is in the middle of the room, with tons of papers scattered all over it. I step closer. Some papers appear to be drawings, blueprints, of an underground layout, very similar to the dungeon where they keep us.

An old photograph of a family portrays a teenage boy with his father and mother. The father and the boy look almost identical. The mother stands barely off from the other two. None of them look happy. Actually, they all look miserable. *Who are they?*

Next, I review the assorted papers. They all have a similar pattern—names, dates, locations, crops.

Huh?

Then, I see my father's name. I pick up this particular document with shaky hands. I try to read, but I don't understand.

DuBois Family:

-Patrick DuBois (age 44), husband of Beatrice DuBois (age 42). One child: Grace DuBois (age 20). No other living relatives.

-Cultivation: strawberries.

-Location: Ponchatoula, Louisiana.

-Total gross income is $20,000 per acre.

-Total acres: 250

-Transportation: railroads to the northern and western regions; maritime through Mississippi River and Gulf of Mexico to various countries.

I choose another document.

Landry Family:

-Stewart Landry (age 41), husband of Wendy Landy (age 40). Two children: Robert Landry (age 17) and Belinda Landry (age 9).

-Cultivation: tobacco.

-Location: St. James, Louisiana.

-Total gross income is $1,500 per acre.

-Total acres: 100

-Transportation: railroads to the northern, western regions, and Mexico; maritime through Mississippi River.

Who is that? As I set that document back on the table, I see another name I recognize.

Guidry Family:
- Charles Guidry, I (deceased), husband of Mary Guidry (died in childbirth). One child: Charles Guidry, II (age 21).
- Cultivation: rice.
-Location: Houma, Louisiana.
-Total gross income is $10,000 per acre.
-Total acres: 84
-Transportation: railroads to the northern, western, and eastern regions, Mexico; maritime through Mississippi River and Gulf of Mexico to various countries.

I drop the paper, and my cheeks flush with anger. Someone researched us all. But who? I need to tell Charles about this. Maybe he has an idea of what the hell all this is about. God, I hope he's ok. I hope he figures out that I've made my way back to the well. *Please come find me.* What if he doesn't?

My mind spins with answers, questions, and next steps. A heaviness weighs in my chest as panic truly sets in. People trying to hurt us, people dying, Charles not showing up, the well, this cottage, these papers—too much information to process.

I bend over, gripping onto the table for dear life to concentrate on my breathing, when the door to the cottage opens.

Oh my god, I'm caught! Where do I go? I can't run and hide. There isn't anywhere to run.

I freeze. My body, panicking mere moments ago, turns to ice. I just stand there as my veins chill from my heart all the way down into my finger tips and the ends of my toes.

A tall man appears in the doorway. Initially, his face is casted downward, but as he enters, his eyes lock with mine. His devilishly handsome face contorts in shock when he sees me.

He looks familiar. Is that the man in the photograph? I want to glance back down at the photo to confirm, but I am mesmerized by his prominent features. His irises are light blue, like ice. They contrast with his black pupils, which dilate for a moment. His eyes alone convey that I should not cross him.

Well, so much for that.

His eyebrows are thick, but not bushy. He has a strong jaw and a pointed nose. He exudes dominance. His hair, slicked back in a stylish, business-like manner, is black like his pupils. His frame fills the doorway. He clears six feet, easily.

"Who the *fuck* are you, and what the fuck are you doing in here?" he boasts. His voice is deep, angry. I'm definitely not supposed to be in here.

I have no idea what to say. My mind is blank. I'm stuck in time and space. I watch his lips move, but my body can't respond.

He steps closer on the other side of the table. "I said, who the fuck are you?"

Closer now, I see that he is young, perhaps early thirties. He wears a black sack suit, perfectly. His figure is tall and slender but not scrawny. He's not too muscular either. He's probably never needed to lift a finger in his whole damned life. I sense entitlement and money, lots of money.

I hate him. Why would his photograph be in this scum hole if he didn't own the place? I can't tell if he is the father or the teenage boy. They look identical, and I have no idea how long ago that photograph was taken.

I still haven't moved or spoken. I probably look deaf and stupid. My lack of response only angers him more. He gives up on me answering as he turns and yells, "Larsen, get the fuck over here. Get this prisoner out of this cottage and back where she belongs!"

Oh no! I don't want to go back! And not with Larsen!

"Please," I finally find my voice. I beg out of panic, not pity. "Please, don't put me back there."

This man whips his head around and shoots daggers with his ice blue and black eyes, questioning my audacity to talk to him now. How can his eyes sparkle with emotion yet appear lifeless at the same time?

"I'll do anything, anything you want. Just please don't let him take me back."

Before he can reply, Larsen appears in the cottage. "Haha, it's you! Ya havin' fun wit' this one yet, Mista Henry?"

"What the fuck are you talking about, Larsen?"

"She's the one I was tellin' ya about. She's the feisty one."

"Well, she doesn't appear feisty right now. She looks like a frightened, annoying little kitten, doesn't she?" Henry stares at me, waiting for me to make a move, testing me. When I don't fall for his scheme, he turns back Larsen. "Take her back to her cell. I don't know how the fuck y'all let her out. You told me the woods were on lock down."

"They are. But she's a smart one."

"Is she now?" Henry looks back to me, intrigued.

"She's been here ove' a week now. She's the longest to survive," Larsen adds to my repertoire. "The others who ha' bin here tha' same amoun' a time as her are already dead."

Their collective gazes make me recoil. They clearly want to eat me alive. Maybe they want to skin me alive. Who knows. I don't know what to do. I feel so disgusted. I can either play their game or return to my hole. I have to pick between the lesser of two evils, of two very bad evils.

I wet my lips before I speak, "I said I'll do anything, and I mean it. I'm sure I could be of some assistance for you. Anything you want. As long as you don't put me back in that cell."

"Where would a prisoner like you stay, then, if not your cell?" Henry prompts, one eyebrow raising.

I say the first answer that pops into my head. "The main house, where you stay."

Henry throws his head back and bellows. He laughs so loudly, he surprises Larsen as well. "How do you know that's where I stay?"

I hate him for what he's done to me and the rest of the prisoners, and he talks to me like I'm some sort of child. He insults my intelligence. I can't hold back my reply. "The way you carry yourself, like you're some self-righteous prick," I declare with spite.

He narrows his eyes at me, and the hatred between us is palpable.

"I tol' ya she's a feisty one," Larsen reminds Henry.

"Punish her. Make her an example for the other prisoners so they see what happens when they escape. Then, take her back to her cell and make sure she doesn't get any food for the rest of the day. I'll see how much longer she survives here," Henry barks and storms out of the cottage.

CHAPTER
14

I MUST BE IN A BAD DREAM. NO, ACTUALLY THIS IS A NIGHTMARE. The kind of nightmare when I wake up sweating, and my face is damp and swollen from crying in my sleep. My heart pounds loudly in my chest. I tell myself to breathe, to calm down. "It was only a dream. It was only a dream. You're awake now. It wasn't real."

Well, this is no dream. This is my new reality. I can't wake myself from this living nightmare. My parents are dead, and I have been captured, tormented, with no escape in sight. My will to survive weakens. And I met the devil himself, the man responsible for this hell.

I just stood there. I couldn't move. This whole time, I told myself that when I met the person responsible for all, I would kill them. I was ready to sacrifice my own life to put them in the grave.

But I just stood there. *Why didn't I do something?*

Oh yeah, I did. I begged. I begged for my pathetic life like a little lost puppy.

Henry is probably still laughing to himself about how scared I looked when he caught me in that cottage. My anger and hatred rise the more I think about him and what I didn't do to him when I had the chance. And now, they will punish me. Well, at least it doesn't sounds like an execution. I will live another day and hope for another chance for revenge.

When we exit the cottage, I discover we are still in the woods, but the trees and the surrounding shrubbery look different. Walking through the secret underground well tunnel, it was hard to tell how much time passed and how far I actually traveled.

Larsen stands in front with his back to me. He approaches a beautiful brown horse with a black mane and tail tied to a nearby tree. *Where is Will?* I thought they do their dirty work together.

"These trees don't look familiar. Where are we?"

Larsen hesitates before answering my question. "We on the othe' side of the property. One in which you wasna suppose' to have access to." He unties the horse before continuing, "How did ya make it ove' to this side? The woods that ya pris'ners wonder 'round are suppose' to be separate from this area here by barb wire an' other traps."

Do I tell him about the well? Would that hurt Charles's possibility for a chance to escape? If I don't tell him, then Larsen can't trust me, maybe reducing my odds of a decent punishment or escape. I don't even know if Charles is still alive.

"There's a well."

"A well, huh?"

He waits for me to continue. I stay silent for a bit, hoping that is enough information to satisfy him.

"Go on," he demands as he waves his hands at me.

"Yes, a well with no water. I climbed down and found a long tunnel at the base that ended with a staircase. I opened the hatch at the top of the stairs, and next thing I know, I step into this cottage." I explain my unexpected escapade in hopes he doesn't think I was trying to escape, at least not yet. I don't deserve punishment for that. I can't help that I magically appeared in a secret cottage.

Larsen lets out a low, gruff chuckle. "Ya brave, climbin' down wells by yerself that you may no' get out of. An' walkin' down pitch-black tunnels. Let see how brave ya are wit' yer punishment, shall we?"

"Where is Will?"

Larsen's shoulders hitch at my question and my continued conversation. Yet, he answers my question, again.

"He's busy a' the moment."

Maybe he does have a soul, just a little. "I thought you usually work together. Are you Henry's lackeys?" I know I'm pushing my luck, but what the hell. They are already punishing me anyway.

"It's best ya keep yer' mouth shut." Yep, I just poked the bear.

I stutter, "I- I'm sorry. I just can't help notice that you have better jobs than the rest of the guards and other servants on the property. I figured you two were more important than the rest." Maybe my swift apology and ego boost will help my situation.

"We all play a role in this here job. He trusts Will and me the mos' ove' the years, I guess. We take care of Mista Henry, an' Mista Henry take care of us."

"Well, he sure as hell doesn't take care of any of us. Does he not see how degrading and inhumane all this is?"

Larsen slaps me with the palm of his hand. *God, that hurt.*

"There's more of tha' ta come. Like I tol' ya already. It's best ta keep that pretty mouth of yers close'. Or it won' just be me punishin' ya later. I'll let Will in on the action too."

He signals for me to mount the horse, and he jumps up behind me, thus ending my fact-finding mission and guiding me back into the unknown.

As the horse gallops through the woods, our journey does not take nearly as long as when I walked the woods with Charles. The secret cottage is deep in the woods on the east side of the estate. That cottage was definitely not supposed to be discovered.

Instead of bringing me back to the hole, Larsen directs the horse closer to the main house on the estate. He climbs down and ties us to a nearby post.

"Stay on the horse. Don' think of doin' anything funny now, ya hear?" he commands me with a clipped tone. Servants and guards are everywhere so there isn't much I could do anyway.

He walks over to a nearby guard and talks to him. The guard runs off immediately, and Larsen returns to help me down from the horse. Even with my feet on the ground, he keeps his grip on my arm.

"Well, well, what hav' we go' here?"

My stomach cringes. I hate the tone of his voice and the way he treats me. Will wipes his face with his dirty, navy-blue bandana. As I watch the bandana cover Will's face, I realize that's not dirt. It's blood. I wonder whose blood. Is my mother's still on there?

"Ya havin' fun wit' 'er yet, Larsen?"

"Not yet, but she's about ta be punish' for tryin' to escape."

"I didn't mean to escape." I look at Larsen with angry eyes.

Will gets in my face. "Since ya 'bout ta be punishe', I won' smack ya cross the face this time. But ya hav' no right ta talk ta me, bitch. Larsen, ya betta keep 'er in line."

"Oh, don't worry, I'm abou' ta hav' my way wit' her."

"You make me sick."

Will suddenly grabs my throat with his big hands and squeezes. He cuts off my airway, and I can't breathe. "Ya gonna die tonight. I'll make sure of it." He squeezes harder before shoving me away. Larsen still held my arm so only half of my body dangles toward the ground as I cough air back into my lungs.

"Will! I needed you ten minutes ago. Where the fuck have you been?"

Trying to breathe, I gaze up to the second-floor balcony. Henry stands with his hands on the rail, casually watching us.

"I'll be righ' there, sir."

"Hurry up! I haven't got all day." Henry turns back inside his house, and Will briskly leaves to tend to his master.

While looking up at the balcony, I notice a woman standing in another window on the same floor. She is dressed in a dark purple gown, and her hair is tied up and held back to showcase her face.

Is that Henry's wife?

I don't remember Henry wearing a wedding ring. But it wasn't like I was looking. The lady seems a bit older though. I'm too far away to decipher other details from her appearance.

She stares back at me. I'm forced to look away first when Larsen pulls on my arm. When I glance back up, she's gone. "Who was that?"

"Ya mean ta tell me ya don' remember Will?"

"No, not him. The lady in the window."

Larsen follows my gaze. "Oh, tha' Mizzus Edith, Henry's mother. Ya don' wanna cross her. If ya think Henry's bad, Mizzus Edith's much worse. She taught him ever'thing he knows," he explains with a smirk.

Henry must be the young teenager in that photograph, then. "Where is Henry's father?"

"Shu' up! An' stop askin' questions. Yer gettin' us bot' in trouble the more ya speak. Ya don' deserve ta hav' answers to yer questions."

We stop walking in front of another hitching post off to the side of the house. The guard that ran off before approaches us with rope.

"Stick ou' yer hands," Larsen commands. I comply. He ties my hands around the post like I'm hugging it. There is a little slack on the post but not enough to move. Then, the guard hands Larsen a belt.

Oh no.

I swallow to hide my fear. This is going to hurt. I can only take so many mental and physical beatings a day. My body still hurts from falling down the well, my side is still sore from the knife fight the day before, and my ankle is still recovering from the unexpected snake bite. I can't count the number of times I was slapped in the face. I hurt. I hope I'll survive this.

Larsen whistles loudly. "We'er ove' here!"

I can't see who he calls. I try to turn my head, but Larsen tied me so I don't have a good radius of motion.

"Ya go' 'em all?" Larsen asks.

"Yes, bu' another died in the woods today. So tha' makes five accounted for an' yers tied up ove' there. Six in all." Another guard answers Larsen.

Who died in the woods today? I hope it wasn't Charles. Maybe he made it out from the other night. Or maybe he is part of the count. I hope he's okay.

The sun is setting. The remaining prisoners must be returning. I hear footsteps behind me and light chatter until a guard yells, "Shut up!"

Larsen's boisterous voice startles me. "Prisoners, before me is one of yer fellow inmates who tried to escape. It's time to make a example of what happens if any of ya attempt this absurd idea of disappearin'."

Before I can give myself a pep talk, a brutal pain radiates across my back. I scream, "*Arrggghh!*" I can't think before another blow comes. "*Ahhhh!*" Tears sting my eyes. Oh. My. God. This hurts so much. *Whack!* The tears now fall, and I don't stop.

Will laughs in the background. My legs shake uncontrollably.

"STOP!" Someone yells.

"No one is stoppin' me, boy." *Whack!*

I drop to the ground, and my arms hang above me as I buckle as low as my restraints allow. I think I might pass out. Actually, I hope I do. I don't want to feel this level of pain anymore.

"I'll take her place! Whip me instead! Let me take her place!" The same voice pleads.

Charles? Am I dreaming? I'm barely conscious, but I think I hear his voice.

"Ya really wanna be tha' stupid, boy?" Larsen questions.

"Yes. Take me instead."

The whipping stops. Larsen starts to untie me. "It's yer lucky day. Someone wants ta get beat too. I get ta beat two of y'all for one of yer mistakes."

I barely hear him. I feel like a rag doll. My hands drop, and my body slumps to the ground. As I lay there, I see the person who took my place.

A guard ties him to the pole, and those green eyes pierce me. Charles stares at me. I can't tell if he's sad or angry. Maybe he looks worried.

"Yer a stupid boy for takin' the place of a pathetic prisoner like 'er," Larsen spits out.

"Charles," I sigh. He is right in front of me yet I can't reach up and touch him.

No one moves me. I'm too weak to move on my own. They let me lay there to watch the assault on Charles. He holds his mouth shut to stifle the torture. As the blows continue, Charles closes his eyes so I cannot look at his suffering.

Larsen doesn't let up either. He strikes him over and over again. I don't know how Charles is able to stand there for as long as he does.

Larsen finally stops. Charles can barely stand so when he is untied, he falls to the ground next to me. His beautiful eyes finally open again and look right into me.

He whispers, "I love you." My chest constricts from his words. I wish I could touch him. I start to lift my hand toward his.

Larsen kicks me. "Get up!"

"Ahh!" I screech. Everything hurts.

"I said, get up!" Larsen grabs me and drags me across the clearing toward the hole.

I use all my energy to glance back at Charles. He still lays there while two guards drag him up also. I wish I could tell Charles I love him back. I wish I met him under different circumstances. I wish we could marry and have children together. I wish for a lot of things I know I will never have.

Larsen throws me into my cell. "Ya lucky yer boyfrien' saved ya," he remarked with a smirk. "Henry an' his mother seem ta enjoy the show." He slams the door, leaving me alone with the thoughts of today's events and new battle wounds to prove it.

How will I survive?

CHAPTER
15

MY MIND IS DELIRIOUS. I HAVEN'T EATEN ANYTHING IN A LONG time. I was almost beaten to death. I think I'm awake, but it's too hard to tell. I'm not sure how much time passes. I drift in and out of consciousness.

A brisk knock at my door brings me back to reality a bit. Once again, another unknown guard stands there with rope to tie my hands. *How many guards do these people have at their beck and call?*

I can't keep doing this. I hate this game. Just kill me already.

I put my head down and stare at the floor, wishing it could swallow me up. An empty pit of despair infests my body. I go numb, first with pain and now from all sense of life. My sense of awareness, touch, smell, and taste disappear. I envision myself falling down the long, dark rabbit hole, just like in *Alice's Adventures in Wonderland.* All logic doesn't exist.

"Hurry up."

I snap out of my absent existence when I hear the guard speak to me. Just when I thought I was gone from this life, my hearing brings me back.

"He's waitin' for ya."

"Who's waiting for me?"

"He doesna like ta be kep' waitin'. Let's go."

Is he talking about Larsen? Or maybe Will? God, I hate Will. Hell, I hate Larsen too, but at least he answers me when I ask him questions, sometimes. Oh no, please don't let it be Theo. I have no energy to prevent his advances toward me.

Anxiety invades my body, and tingling pains that shoot down to my fingers and toes return me back to life. My airways constrict from the tight sleeve that seems to permanently reside over my heart.

Who is waiting for me?

I need to just get this over with. I know this guard won't answer me. I am sore and hurt from yesterday. Hell, from every day. Every body part aches. How much more can I take?

I slowly reach a seated position. Just performing that task makes me light headed. I slide to the closest wall and grip it for support as I attempt to rise on my feet. The guard allows me to take my time. I drag my feet and make my way to the guard. I huff in discomfort with every step and breath I take.

Finally, I lift my hands as high as they can go. The weight of his stare tells me I'm in really bad shape. I don't need a mirror to prove it. He grasps my hands together and raises them up another couple of inches. I want to collapse in his arms, and he can carry me the rest of the way.

He ties my hands, grabs my arm, and leads me up the stairs out of the hole. I groan in pain. *Would everyone stop grabbing my arm?* I'm too weak to run off anyway.

"I'm tryin' ta help ya walk. I don' think yad make it out on ya own," he explains.

I guess I can accept that. Although I don't like it. I hate this damn dungeon—the smell, the flickering lights, the memories. Getting out of here motivates me a little, even if I don't know who I am about to see.

There is no one waiting at the clearing. The guard continues to carry our strides in the opposite direction from the woods.

"Where are you taking me?" I moan.

"Where does it look like I'm takin' ya?"

Smart ass. Eventually, in front of us looms the main house. My fate must lie in there.

A butler greets us on the back patio with a bow. "Good morning. I'll take her from here." The guard releases my arm, and as soon as I demonstrate I can stand on my own, he leaves me and walks back toward the clearing. "This way, miss," the butler spins on his fancy shoes and quickly steps inside the house.

"Can you untie me?" I ask. I might as well try. I have nothing left, except a prayer. He doesn't respond. He doesn't even look back to acknowledge me. So much for that request then.

I follow him, as quickly as my feet allow, down a massive hallway. When we reach a doorway, he turns to face me. I am a few paces behind him, but he waits for me to approach. He reaches for my hands, unties the rope, and ushers me inside the beautiful parlor.

Each wall contains hand-painted murals. Multiple cream couches sit next to matching chairs, all with accents of dark brown wood for the legs and arm rests. A table in the center hosts bread and other decadent treats. I'm tempted to reach over and stuff my face because I'm so hungry. But something isn't right here.

The butler startles me when he speaks, "Please have a seat wherever you like. He will be right in."

I turn to ask him *who is he*, but the butler is gone and the door already shut. I feel so out of place in my shambled state. I'm afraid to sit down and dirty the cream couch. I decide to walk around the room and look at the murals and pictures hanging on the walls. I keep glancing at the food.

Is it even real?

"Please, help yourself."

I look up at the deep voice. It's *him*. Henry dominates the room. He just stands there, staring at me.

"Don't make me repeat myself. I know you're hungry, so help yourself."

I don't like to be commanded and barked at like a dog. I want that food more than anything right now, but I will do so in on my own time.

"Do you have any plates?" I ask.

His brows quirks. "You don't need a plate to eat the food that's in front of you."

"Would you use a plate?"

"That is irrelevant."

"I beg to differ."

"How so?"

"You've given me crap food in that cell like a dog, and I had to eat like one. Now that I am in this house, eating normal food, I choose to eat like a human. I request a plate."

Henry offers a sinister smile. He waits a few moments, long enough that I want to squirm under his gaze, but I hold my head high. "I was told you were a feisty one. I couldn't wait to experience it for myself."

"I hope I haven't disappointed you."

His smile widens, showing his straight, white teeth. If I didn't hate him so much, I would find him very attractive. "Marcel!"

The butler arrives in no time. "Yes, Mister Henry?"

"Please bring Miss ..." Henry's voice trails off and glances back at me.

"Grace," I say strongly so he won't forget my name, not after everything he has done to me.

"Please bring Miss Grace a plate and a glass of water."

"Actually, I'll have some scotch instead." If I face punishment or, worse, murder, I want to enjoy one more glass of scotch before I die.

The butler doesn't move, waiting for his master's orders. Henry keeps his eyes fixed on me the entire time.

"Bring us two glasses of scotch." Marcel leaves and Henry and I are alone again. "A scotch drinker, huh?"

"Yes."

"Any other surprises I need to know about?"

"Tons."

Henry laughs as he takes a seat in one of the single chairs. Marcel returns shortly with my plate and our scotch. "That is all, Marcel." Henry dismisses the butler, who closes the door behind him. Henry gestures with his hand. "Please, sit."

Does he not notice that my filthy clothes will ruin his pristine furniture?

"I do not like to repeat myself." He stares at me with a stern look.

"I'll sit, but not because you demanded. I choose to sit because it's a burden for me to stand any longer," I quip.

Henry covers his mouth with a hand to hide his smirk.

I sit on the cream couch and lean over to select some items from the food table. I consider not using my plate at all, just to prove a point, but I figure since I was given what I asked for, I'll play nice and perhaps gain more leverage.

I take my time surveying the food to feign self-control. I choose only a few items to start. I carefully eat the grapes one by one and examine each to see if they pass my inspection before indulging them.

Henry watches my every move. He crosses one leg over the other and rests one hand under his chin while the other holds his scotch. His gaze is calculating, yet with a hint of intrigue and perhaps…desire.

"Why am I here?" *Why am I here right now? Why am I at this estate at all? Why do you have prisoners? And why are we all locked up playing a stupid game?*

"You begged me to help you. You said you would do anything for me."

I swallow my next bite of food with a big gulp. I tentatively reply, "Yes, I did." Maybe I should regret that decision, but I relish eating and drinking like a human being. I can't help but want to feel normal again.

"I want you." My eyes snap to his. "You intrigue me, and everyone else here that encounters you seems to feel the same way. And I'm the only one who can ultimately control you. I find that very thrilling. You will be at my beck and call, whenever and however I want you. Do you understand?"

Well, straight to the point then.

I take a long drink of my scotch, replaying Henry's words in my mind. I hate him. He disgusts me. But I don't really seem to have any other choice. There is no alternative. Yet my blood boils.

"No one controls me," I snark.

"Prove it."

He's right. I don't have any rights or freedom here. Not yet. I must build trust with him too. I can't believe I'm about to do this. "On one condition."

Henry smirks again, amused by our banter.

"I stay here in the house with you. I eat like a human. I'm treated like a human. I bathe like a human, and I dress like a lady."

"I believe that is more than one condition."

Prick.

"I shouldn't be treated any differently than you while staying in this house. I hardly think you want a smelly maiden or an unfed skeleton in your bed. I need to be close to you when you call for me, which is why I request to stay in the house. I'm sure you have more than enough rooms to accommodate me."

I want to vomit. This is what I must do to survive.

He drinks, raising his scotch slowly, still assessing me with his dark eyes. Then, he stands. Is he leaving? The recurring panic starts to settle in my chest.

"Fine. Dinner is at six thirty sharp. You are to meet me in the dining room at that time. Lunch will be served in your room, shortly. Make sure you are washed up and presentable for tonight."

Just like that, he abruptly leaves the room. I finally exhale the breath I held since he entered the parlor.

What have I really agreed to?

CHAPTER
16

HE LEFT ME ALONE. I SHOVE FOOD IN MY MOUTH AND KICK back the rest of my scotch.

My first impression of Henry at the secret cottage was one of a huge asshole. The guards also warned how mean he can be. I even witnessed a small part of his anger and impatience. However, just now, he said "please" to his butler and honored all my requests. I can't help but feel that underneath such a hard exterior, Henry may have more to him than what meets the eye.

He's such a gorgeous, vile prick. I think of the various sexual activities he will require, and my mind turns to Charles. I must survive this for us. Maybe somehow I can make my way back to the hole and help him escape. I miss him so much. I still can't believe Charles took the rest of my punishment.

The door opens again, breaking my reverie. "Hanna!"

"Sure nice to see ya again, Miss Grace."

"What are you doing here?"

"Imma here to bring ya up to get clean an' dress. Looks like ya need it. So follo' me."

Hanna leads me out of the parlor and down another the long hallway toward a staircase. Hanna walks slowly, which allows my lethargic pace to keep up. On the second floor, we pass multiple doors, many open to bedrooms.

What kind of events do they host? They can accommodate so many guests for the night. Or maybe these rooms are used for..... other ominous activities. This could be where he keeps his company, his other prisoners.

Jesus.

Has he done this before? Does his mother know? Of course she knows. She apparently enjoyed the show of my punishment. Larsen said she is worse than Henry. They have to be in this together, whatever *this* is. Hence why there are so many guards and servants. This doesn't seem new to anyone around here.

What sick and twisted people—all of them—except maybe Hanna. But I can't fully trust her yet either.

No one here will help me or any of the other prisoners, not to escape or even just survive. Something big must be going on, especially to have this many people working here. I need to figure it out. I'm in this alone.

No, Charles is with me. I need to find him, if he is even still alive. We will figure this out together and leave here. Hopefully along the way, we can make restitution for what we endured.

Hanna stops at the last room on the right. She unlocks the door with a key and walks in first. I take in the monstrous room before me and reflect on all my prior philosophies of this place. Then I see the bed. Oh, how I miss sleeping in a bed! My instincts carry forward, and I imagine sprawling on top of the covers. I want to sleep for hours and give my mind the rest it deserves.

My hand reaches out to run along the bedspread when I notice how disgusting I am, beyond disgusting actually. Without proper hygiene and sanitation, my hand looks black, compared to the stark white sheets. I quickly pull my hand away. I need to clean myself off first. I need to clean off *everything* from me.

Hanna reappears from a room attached to the bedroom. I hear water running and pray to God for it to be a bathroom. The sound gets louder as I approach and discover an upscale porcelain bathtub.

"Take off ya dress and get in."

Gladly. This is one command I will obey. I remove my clothes without hesitation and climb into the beautiful tub. The water temperature is perfect. This is real!

Hanna returns holding a bar of soap. She begins to wash me when I hear her gasp. "Chil'! Wha' happen ta ya!" She gently traces the lines on my back. It's still tender from yesterday, and it burns from the soap. But it feels so good to wash my body.

"Please help me wash it all away," I beg.

Hanna stays silent as she bathes me from head to toe. This peaceful moment is likely the only time I will have for myself after tonight. I wish this moment could last forever. After she rinses the soap from my skin, Hanna grabs a towel and helps me out of the tub.

"Do I have to get out? I'm not ready yet."

"Yes, ya are ready, chil'. I'll make sure ya get a good lunch. Ya need ta fatten up, like me."

I chuckle. I wouldn't mind laying down in the bed to wait for more food.

I doze off for God knows how long. It was the most amazing nap I've ever had in my entire life. When I open my eyes, I notice a plate of food next to the bed.

This feels like heaven.

Unfortunately, I remind myself that I'm really in hell. The devil will now consume me during the length of my stay here in the main house.

Once again, I scarf down all the food without leaving a crumb in sight. Henry must have told someone that my drink of choice is scotch because there, next to the empty plate, is a glass with two fingers of scotch. *Is this a joke?* Henry is playing mind games. He doesn't care about me, or anyone for that matter. He locks me up in that hell hole for a whole week and now he gives me scotch.

Bastard.

I gladly take the scotch and down the contents swiftly. I welcome the burn as it trails down my throat and coats my stomach. I rest my head back onto the pillow and close my eyes. I think of my father and mother. I want to successfully escape for them. However, I now have a new objective: get Charles out. I need to figure out a way to escape *with* Charles.

I don't want to do this alone. For as long as Charles is in the hole, half of my heart is there too. We need to leave together for me to feel complete again. The burning desire to succeed fills me more than that plate of food. Someone other than myself is counting on me to survive.

I decide to explore the house. I can make a mental map of where I am and potential escape routes. I can observe where and how the servants and guards operate, know their routines, and find a weak spot in the system.

I reach the door and grasp the handle to open it. But it doesn't move. I try it again, yanking harder this time. The door is locked.

Shit.

I rest my forehead on the door. "Think, Grace." I command myself. I turn around and check to see if I can open any of the windows. I try to lift each one with no luck. "The bastard locked me in here!"

The reality crawls over my skin like dozens of spiders, and my chest constricts. I just traded one cage for another. Rage blinds me, and with my liquid courage, I bang on the door.

"Let me out! Let me out!"

After a few moments, the lock on the door turns. I back away but continue to breathe heavily with rabid anger that I am about to unleash on Henry. I want full range of the house, just like I asked.

Except Henry doesn't answer the door. It's Hanna.

"Hanna, please get me out of here." I make my way back to the door to leave the room.

But Hanna is too quick. She slams the door closed and locks it from the inside this time. She stands in front of the door. "Chil', are ya crazy?"

"I'm not the crazy one. *He* is! *You* are! All of you!" I start to cry. God, I hate crying. Before coming here, I never cried. My mother always took care of me and made everything better. But she's not here anymore.

Hanna hugs me. "Shhh now. It'll be ok, chil'. Stop cryin'." She brushes the hair out of my face and looks me in the eyes. "Ya need ta look presentable for dinna. We gonna fin' ya an outfit for tonight. An' Imma show ya need yer rest for later. So go on an' lay down an' try ta fall back 'sleep. I'll wake ya in time to get dress for dinna soon."

I have no choice and nowhere to go. So I lay down in my inebriated state and return to slumber.

CHAPTER
17

I WAKE UP TO NOISE, BUT I DON'T WANT TO OPEN MY EYES YET. I HAVE a light headache from the multiple scotch drinks. I used to drink with my father almost every night either at dinner or before bed. Now I'm a light weight. Plus, losing weight since my arrival made the effects from alcohol pretty potent.

I have to be careful. I have to be alert. I also need water. I slowly open my eyes and find Hanna bustling around the room.

"'Bout time ya woke up." She hands me a glass. "Go on an' drink. Ya look like ya went ta hell an' back."

"I am in hell," I croak. I savor the taste of the fresh water.

"M'ster Henry'll be upset if ya not fit for dinna."

"I don't give a damn about Henry." Hanna flashes a nasty look on her face. I think she worries for her own safety, not mine. The last thing I want to do is get Hanna in trouble, especially since she's somewhat helped me through all this shit as best as she could. "I'll be fine. Don't worry."

"Ya betta. Now let see 'ere. Get in ya dress, an' I'll fix ya hair."

I take one last look in the vanity mirror and stare at someone I do not recognize anymore. My hair is pulled back in a half up, half down fashion with loose curls down my back. I wear a pale pink chiffon dress with a low neckline that turns right at the shoulders. The sleeves droop down the arms and wrap around right at the elbows. The bodice is tight around the waist and loosens below my waist all the way down to the floor with a small train to follow. Accents of a gold lace pattern swirl around the bosom, sleeves, and bottom rim of the dress.

I look beautiful, young, healthy. I catch a glimpse of my past life, one to which I can never return. Now I must play the role of a harlot.

"You can do this." I calm myself, trying to breathe through the sudden nausea. I place a fake smile on my face and, with a little more determination, repeat, "You can do this."

I follow Hanna down the stairs. My heartbeat echoes with each step I take toward the unknown. Down the hallway, I take a deep breath as she opens two French-style doors, and the astonishing dining room is revealed to me.

A gorgeous chandelier hangs in the middle of the room above the massive table that could easily seat thirty people at one time. Multiple buffet style tables rest along the perimeter containing various china, stemware, silver, and crystal.

But I am most surprised by the female sitting at the other end of the table, watching me. Her face mirrors my own shock.

"Um…hello."

She stares at me for several moments, as if I did not speak to her directly. She must remember we are alone in the room, though, as she replies, "Oh, um, hi there." Her thick accent tells me she's from Mississippi.

I remember a boy years ago who traveled to my house to court me. He and his father had a few days journey from his house to mine in Ponchatoula. I'll never forget his thick accent. He was from

Mississippi. They had an indigo plantation in Natchez. Obviously, it didn't work out between us.

"Who are you?" I ask.

"I'm Annabel. I thought you were dead."

"Excuse me?"

"I saw you getting whipped. You fell, and then the other prisoner took your spot. You just laid there. I thought you were dead when they took you away because you didn't move."

My mouth gapes open. "Are you a prisoner, like me?"

"Yes."

There are two of us here? "Why are you here?" Is she here for the same reasons I am? I wonder if she knows.

"I'm not exactly sure. I was brought into the house earlier by a servant. I was given a bath, and a maid changed my clothes and styled my hair. She said I was to eat dinner in the main house. That's all I know."

She doesn't know my arrangement then. I'd like to keep it my dirty little secret.

"Do you know what's going on?" she asks timidly.

Should I tell her what I've discovered? No, probably not. She looks scared enough as it is. I think it's best if I play innocent like her. "No, I—"

"Hello, ladies." Henry's deep voice echoes in the room, cutting me off from my lies to Annabel. He walks around me to the side opposite where Annabel is seated. He continues to stand and gestures his hands toward Annabel. "Grace, take a seat next to..." Henry holds his words in the air, waiting on Annabel's response.

"Annabel," she answers.

"Annabel. Grace, take a seat next to Annabel." I roll my eyes. I slowly make my way over to the other side of the massive table. Why did she have to sit so far away? I defiantly leave an empty seat between us. There are about twenty-nine other chairs, after all.

I catch Henry's smirk before he wipes it from his face.

"Dinner is ready so I will just get to the point so we can eat. I'm sure y'all are hungry."

Asshole. Of course we are.

"I brought you both here for my benefit only. Both of you will be summoned when I need you, for anything. Sometimes, it may just be one of you, and sometimes it may be both. I expect you to follow my orders without a quarrel. While you serve me, you are to stay in this house and enjoy the meals prepared for you, like tonight for instance. If you do not wish to participate in my offer, then I will send you back underground just like before. Do I make myself clear?"

Wow. Can he be more of a prick? I guess one prisoner isn't good enough. He needs another girl to play with, too. All this is a sick game for him, and I'm a pointless player.

Henry's face reddens. We haven't answered him. I think Annabel is trying to comprehend all the information just presented to her. Poor girl.

I'm the one who suggested this whole charade to get me out the hole so I shouldn't need to agree to my own proposal. However, he changed the rules on me. Damn him. I cross my arms and glance over at Annabel.

Annabel swallows audibly, "So when you say anything, do you mean sexually too?"

Henry lays his hands on the table and leans closer. "Yes. When I say anything, I mean just that. Anything."

"Oh," she whispers. She looks down at her hands folded in her lap.

I wonder how long she's been here or how she's been treated. Maybe she and I can work together while we stay here.

To give her confidence, I answer first. "I'll do it." I look directly in Henry's eyes.

He smiles. "Annabel?"

"Um, sure. Yes, I guess."

"Great. That's settled. Now let's eat."

Henry sits across from us. The servants bring turtle soup for the first course to dinner. The smell is delicious, and I am pleasantly surprised to see I am given a spoon as well. Such a small gesture makes me happy these days.

I patiently wait for all three of us to be served before I eat, but Annabel digs into her bowl like she is starving. I can't blame her. I'm tempted to act the same way, but my mother didn't raise a savage.

Just as Henry receives his bowl of soup, Marcel enters the room, bows, and announces, "Sir, your mother is here to join you for dinner."

"Oh, Christ." Henry throws down his napkin and stands to greet the woman gliding into the room. In walks the lady I saw in the window the day before.

CHAPTER
18

Mrs. Edith is dressed in a beaded, lace black gown from neck to toe. She is fully covered, like a closed book. Her veil of no emotion is only disturbed by her disbelief when she sees me and my fellow companion.

Is that what I call Annabel? Prisoner or harlot sound so degrading. I think companion suits fine.

"Mother," Henry says with a clipped tone.

"I didn't realize you had *guests* in the house." She emphasizes the word like she just ate a sour grape. However, she maintains her poise, despite the disappointment.

"That is none of your concern at the moment. However, since they will be staying here over the next few days, I'll introduce you."

"No bother. I'm not interested in knowing your whores' names."

My eyes flash at her, wishing they can shoot daggers. I hate Mrs. Edith. Even if she didn't kill my parents and take part in locking me up and torturing me, I still hate her. She sticks her nose in the air like she is better than everyone else. One day, her time will come.

"Henry, what are you trying to accomplish with these…" she looks between me and Annabel, "tainted commoners. " One side of her lips tips up in a sneer.

"Don't worry, Mother. This thing with them won't interfere with anything we are doing here. It never has before. Trust me."

"It better not. We've worked too hard to get to this point. Don't blow it."

Working too hard for what? It sounds like they have done this before. My stomach, sadly, doesn't feel like eating much anymore.

The servants bring another soup for Mrs. Edith as she takes her place at the other end of the long table. Annabel practically licked her bowl clean, and Henry reaches for his spoon to continue to eat. When his mother reaches for her spoon, I reach for mine as well.

Mrs. Edith's eyes look over at me. "You shouldn't have waited on my account. I wouldn't have waited for you."

"My mother raised me with manners," I spit back. Henry's eyes shift back and forth between us with amusement.

"Too bad your mother can't teach you any more life lessons, now can she?"

Fucking bitch.

If I had a knife at this table, I would slash her throat in a heartbeat. Two can play this game.

"Not any more than Henry's father, I suppose." I don't know anything about Henry's father, other than Larsen telling me to stop asking questions. His warning didn't seem right at the time, but, again, how would I know?

Henry abruptly stands so fast that his chair falls back on the floor behind him. "Get out!" His ice blue eyes bore into me, and he points to the door. "Get the fuck out of my sight."

Yikes! I definitely hit a nerve. I really don't give a damn about Henry or his father. But my mother deserves respect, even from the grave.

"Gladly." I toss my napkin on the table, stand, and make my way to leave. Unfortunately, I have to pass Mrs. Edith as her seat is closest to the doors.

She continues to eat without acknowledging my leave. As I walk by, though, she grabs my arm. Startled by the intrusive grip, I halt and look down at her. It was hard to make out the details of her face from across the table, but now I can see the wrinkles formed on her pale skin. Her hair is black as night, blacker than Henry's, with only a few grey strands.

Her firm, tight grip demonstrates her strength, contrasting her fragile, thin frame. She emits an evil so grave that even the devil himself would shake in his lair. In another life, I wouldn't want to cross her either. But the past is gone. She is my enemy, and evidently, I am hers.

She continues to stare at me with stern, cold eyes. "You won't survive here much longer. I'll make sure of it."

I am unfazed by her depravity, "That's what everyone keeps telling me. But I'm still here, staying in the same house you are."

Her grip tightens, "I'll make sure you go back to that hell hole where you belong."

"I'll see you there, in hell."

I yank my arm from her grip and storm out of the dining room. I don't even know where the hell I'm going in this dreadful house, as long as it's far away from her. I walk briskly down one of the long hallways, hoping it leads to the stairwell to my room. I try to find my bearings, but all I see is red and Mrs. Edith's blackness.

"Grace!" I snap out of my trance and turn to see Henry chasing after me.

Shit.

He is about to throw me out of this house, back to the hole. I could try to save myself, but he just witnessed everything. Should I apologize? Fuck, no. These people are crazy. I can't apologize for the fact that they killed my parents. Every one of them can go to hell. I'm definitely keeping my mouth shut.

Henry approaches me, likely reading the tumultuous emotions—rage, confusion, fear—flowing through my eyes. "Be ready in your room in thirty minutes. I want you naked, sprawled out on your bed, waiting for me. Do not defy me, or I swear to god I will put you back in your cell." Then, he quickly turns back toward the dining room.

My face is blank. My mind holds no response. *What did I just do?* I hope I'm not about to receive another punishment.

I aimlessly walk around in search of the staircase to the second floor.

I finally make it back to my room, jittery, shaken, nervous. I slowly remove my dress and undergarments. I also let my hair down, hanging and loose around my shoulders. My hearts starts to race as I stand naked in front of the bed, picturing what might happen here in just a few minutes.

At first, my mind took me to a place of punishment. That is all I know of these people. But after wandering back to the room, I believe Henry wants something else from me.

Tonight will be my first time. This is not the way I thought I would lose my virginity. I had hoped it would be out of love, for my husband, on my wedding night. Maybe for Charles. God, I miss him.

My eyes fill with tears. I wish he was the one here about to make love to me. I feel a bit like I'm cheating on him. I quell my thoughts and crawl on the bed.

I assume my position on the comfortable bed. I lay on my back, looking up at the ceiling, with my legs apart and my arms covering my chest. I feel vulnerable—too vulnerable. I close my eyes and concentrate on my breathing.

Eventually, my door opens. I keep my eyes closed. I can't open them. I don't want to look at Henry's face when he sees me.

"Don't cover yourself up. Show me." Henry's deep, commanding voice penetrates the quiet room.

Reluctantly, I move my arms away from my chest and rest them by my sides.

"Take you right hand and touch your clit."

My eyes fly open. *Is he talking to me?* But he is alone.

"You heard me. Do it." He makes his way toward the bed and starts to unbutton his shirt.

I close my eyes again. I don't exactly know what I'm doing.

"Don't make me say it again, or I will punish you."

I glide my right hand across my stomach down between my legs. I feel uneasy. But just like he commanded, I touch my clit very softly back and forth.

"Good. Rub your clit in circles, slowly."

I concentrate on my fingers, trying to tune out Henry's voice. Instead, I imagine Charles talking to me. I envision his green eyes and handsome smile. I start to feel my fingers getting wet. My breathing becomes shallow.

"Now, take your left hand and rub your left breast. Yes, just like that. Pinch your nipple."

I can feel my body start to tingle. I adjust my legs on the bed from this unfamiliar feeling. Tension leaves my body. I relax into the rhythm of my hand movements. I almost forget I'm not alone in this bedroom, until I hear Henry remove his trousers.

I keep my eyes closed. I'm afraid to lose my confidence and break the role playing. I need to keep thinking of Charles. My body flushes with warmth. My fingers are slick now, and my circles grow faster. The bed dips down a bit from Henry's body weight.

"Slow down. You are not allowed to come yet."

I open my eyes, frustrated with him and his commands. "You're such a prick."

Henry chuckles deeply. "Don't test me. I will do nasty things to that mouth of yours to keep you quiet."

Repulsive.

"Now, flip over, and get on your knees."

Reluctantly, I do what I'm told. As I turn around, Henry's face drops suddenly.

"What happened?"

He must see the marks on my back. "You saw my whipping—"

"No, not that. This..." He gently rubs my side.

I still bear the long slash on my side from the attack of the fellow prisoner. It's only been two days yet it heals with each passing day.

"Oh that." I feel self-conscious about all of my marks suddenly. I am a survivor. But I'm naked in front of a stranger who is evaluating my marred body.

"Yes, that. I asked you a question, and I expect an answer."

"Another prisoner tried to kill me."

Henry runs his fingers down my side along the scar. Although he uses the slightest touch, I feel the soreness still. I try not to grimace from the pain, but his gaze finds my face. He stares with concern in his eyes, for such a brief moment, and then it's gone.

"What?"

"Nothing." His face shutters, devoid of emotion.

"You're lying."

He hesitates before declaring, "I've never met anyone like you."

"That's too bad. Everyone must be boring then."

He laughs. "Your strong, like my mother."

"Don't you dare compare me to your mother."

"Why? You don't like her?" he questions with a knowing grin.

"I hate her, actually."

"You don't know her," he counters on a serious note.

"You don't know me." I match his tone.

"Hmm, maybe that's true. But one day I will." He pauses for a moment, and his voice turns dark. "And I will break you."

"You can't break me. You and your minions had the chance all last week. Even my fellow prisoners tried."

"Again, don't test me, sweet girl."

"You know there is nothing sweet about me."

"I don't actually know you, do I? You just said so yourself."

This circular discussion is exhausting. "Precisely, you don't," I concede.

"Well, since that's settled, get back on your hands and knees."

CHAPTER 19

THAT NIGHT, HENRY TOOK MY VIRGINITY. HE DIDN'T CARE THAT he hurt me the multiple times we had sex. He actually seemed pleased at the blood on the sheets.

Sadist.

He left my room in the early hours of the morning when he was finished with me. I laid in the dirty sheets for only a few minutes before Hanna came to change the evidence. I hope she doesn't think any less of me.

She doesn't say a word the whole time making my bed new again. I don't volunteer any information either. I visit the bathroom and clean myself up, taking my time, hiding as long as it takes for Hanna to finish up and leave.

After she leaves, I return to the bedroom and stare at the bed. All remnants of last night are erased. I wish they could be erased from my memory too.

But I can't change the past. I crawl between the clean sheets and force my eyes closed. I try not to remember what happened here with Henry.

Eventually, my mind fades into darkness.

"Get up, chil'. I canna let ya sleep all day."

"What time is it?"

"Ya miss breakfas', but I won' let ya miss lunch too. Get dress an' come down stairs for lunch in the dinin' room."

I roll over to climb down off the bed. *Ow!* My lady parts are sore. I feel like I can't even walk right now.

"Ya ok?" Hanna asks, concerned.

"Um, yes. I think I'll be fine." I slowly walk over to Hanna, who holds out a light blue dress.

"Ya sure don' look fine ta me."

"Is it supposed to hurt this much?" I blurt. She understood what happened here last night. I'm not sure if Hanna's ever had sex before, but I don't have my mother to ask these kinds of questions anymore.

She pauses, stunned by my question. "When it's ya firs' time, yessum."

"So it gets better, eventually?"

"Sometimes. It hurts less ove' time, an' when the man knows what he's doin', it may even feel good," she explains with a smile and twinkle in her eyes.

No way. "Well, right now, I can't really imagine that."

While Hanna dresses me, I think that she just has to help me escape one day. Every time I ask her, she turns me down. I have grown to like her over time and recognize that she doesn't agree what is entirely going on here.

No matter if I had more information about what is going on here, it doesn't change my current situation. Whatever this is, it is too big for me to take on alone. I can't help but to wonder, though. If I can't trust Hanna, then there really is no person here who cares about me, or any of us here.

"Hanna, one day, I am going to escape this dreadful place." She fixes my dress, acting like she doesn't hear me. "And when I do, I am going to need your help. When that time comes, will you help me?"

She continues to fiddle with my dress, avoiding my eyes.

"I know you hear me. I just want you to know that I can't do this alone. I need you."

Her silence wounds me. I don't expect her to sacrifice herself for me or anything, but I hoped for a sliver of assurance that I'm not alone. But, of course, she works for Henry and his mother. They would likely torture or kill her, if either discovered her as my accomplice. I guess I can't blame her. I'm the one with nothing to lose.

She straightens back up. "Ya ready for lunch. Ya go down there an' fatten ya belly up now." She walks around me and continues to the doorway out of sight.

My eyes water as I fight tears. No one cares about me here, only Charles. I need to get to him as fast as I can before it's too late.

I step into the dining room for lunch with slightly puffy eyes. I couldn't help the few tears that streamed down my face earlier.

Instantly, the aroma of lunch lifts my mood. An assortment of sandwiches, fruit, and desserts are spread on the table. An empty plate by itself makes me chuckle. I grab the plate and serve myself.

Just as I sit to eat, Henry walks in. "Ah, I see you stole my plate."

"You mean *my* plate." I stand my ground.

"Well, that may seem so, but you're wrong. No bother, though. Marcel will bring out another. Marcel!"

"Yes, master?"

"Bring out two more plates, please."

"Of course, sir."

Marcel spins on his fancy shoes to follow orders.

"You need two plates?"

"No, I just need one. But our other guest may like a plate, just like you. Who knows?"

For Annabel? Perhaps his mother. I sure hope not. I won't enjoy my lunch in her presence. "Are you talking about Annabel or your mother?" I ask as I take a seat.

Henry offers me an evil smile, "Wouldn't you like to know? Tell me, if it was my mother, would you leave the dining room?"

Without hesitation, I answer, "Yes."

"I see. That's disappointing because I would love to watch another one of your spats with her." Henry sighs and starts to pile food onto his plate. "Unfortunately, there will be no excitement at the lunch table today. If Annabel cares to join us, the extra plate is available for her."

Whew.

I eat quietly. After last night, it honestly feels a little weird to be in Henry's presence.

"How are you feeling?"

"Excuse me?" Why does he care about how I feel? He definitely didn't care last night.

"You heard me."

"Well, you need to clarify as to what part of me you're talking about. I'm pretty sure my whole damn body hurts."

He chuckles. "You make a good point. Specifically, your cunt. How does it feel?"

What a degrading word. My fingers twitch with anger. "I don't need to tell you how my lady parts feel. You can figure that one out on your own."

"You are a virgin, or I should rather say *were* a virgin."

"Is that a question?"

"No, just an observation. I figured since last night was your first time and you skipped breakfast this morning, you were more than likely sore and in some pain. I'm surprised to see you at lunch actually."

"Well, I guess my hunger won out over my injuries." I won't give this sadist the satisfaction that he inflicted pain on me. I have encountered and conquered many other obstacles. I want my pride intact as much as possible.

"I guess, maybe next time, I'll just have to be that much harder on you."

I avoid his gaze, to hide my rage. I ate enough, I decide. I stand up from the table and place my napkin next to my plate. I push my chair back and start to walk away. I need some distance from him.

"Leaving so soon?" Henry mocks me.

"You're an asshole." I snap over my shoulder and approach the door.

"No, it's your asshole I'll be playing with next, sweetheart. Get yourself ready," he claims.

Oh. My. God. I quickly leave the room. I have nowhere to go, except back to my room, and I don't want to relive the tormenting memories from last night just yet.

Perhaps I can begin to establish a mental map of this place in my head for a potential escape route. Servants mill about. Any one of them can yell out, claiming I am trying to leave. Who knows what will happen to me then.

I settle for casually walking down one of the long hallways while I peer my head around the corners of rooms, hoping to find some privacy and make myself disappear, even if for a few minutes. As I meander by several closed doors, I hear something, more like *someone.*

"Ya los', bitch?"

Fury, already so close to the surface, flows through me that causes my head to ignite like fire. I turn around to confront him.

"Do I look lost, Will?" I'm not lost, but I can't exactly tell him my plans of scouting out an escape route.

"Ya look like ya tryin' ta leave."

"Where could I even go?"

Will walks toward me with his hands behind his back. His false sense of composure keeps me on high alert. I know he hates me. The feeling is mutual. Every time, Will manages to put his hands on me. His hands are behind his back now doesn't mean I can relax, not one bit.

"I know where I woul' put ya. Back in the dungeon where ya belong. Ya no' suppose' ta be 'ere."

He comes even closer. Every part of my body itches from his proximity, telling me to run. But I can't move. "You can't do anything to me, Will. Henry will make sure of it."

The bile rises in my throat with those words. I hope that Will doesn't see through my farce and considers Henry my ally. I don't want to keep looking over my shoulder every time I walk down this hallway.

Will looms over my smaller frame. He leans his face next to mine. His bloody bandana brushes my cheek, and I turn my head to avoid the pungent smell. He whispers in my ear, "I'll see 'bout that. Master Henry may take a likin' ta ya, but I'm sho Mizzus Edith has othe' plans for ya."

Mrs. Edith.

That evil woman has no soul. Even if I manage to win Henry over, I'll never live out of the shadows of Mrs. Edith's presence. Her toxic force drains the life of everything around her. This is no idle threat.

"Ya betta run along an' go back up ta ya room now. Tha's where ya belong. Or I'll call ou' ta Master Henry and Mizzus Edith an' tell 'em ya tryin' ta escape. We'll see what happens ta ya then."

I hate this place. I hate Henry and his mother. There really is nowhere I can go so I turn away from Will and walk up the stairs to my room. Along the way, I pass by multiple doors before reaching mine. Behind one, I hear muffled crying.

I pause to listen at the door and glance around to make sure I'm alone. I reach for the handle, and surprisingly, the door opens.

Annabel lays on her bed, sobbing. *Why isn't her door locked, like mine?* I need to ask Henry about that later. Or maybe I shouldn't.

"Annabel? It's me, Grace."

She lifts her head up and looks at me through her tears. "Grace? What are you doing here?"

"I heard you and came to check on you. Why are you crying?" Did he take her virginity too?

"This sounds silly, but I had the most amazing sleep in a long time. I dreamt I was back home in my life before here. And when I woke up, I realized that I'm far away from home, and I may never see my family again."

"How long have you been crying?"

"All morning. I woke up not that long ago and saw a maid walking down the hall. I asked to eat lunch in my room. I can't go down there looking like this." Red patches cover her face from crying, with puffy eyes and a runny nose, and her hair looks flattened and tangled.

This may be my only chance to talk to her alone, especially before the maid returns with her meal.

"Listen to me, Annabel. I need you to quiet down." Her lip quivers, but her gaze is direct. "You and I can work together to escape. I'm not sure how or when, but we have each other. I think we can take advantage of a situation if one arises."

Her eyes flicker with...is it hope? "Do you think we really can?"

"I don't know. But we have to try."

She sits quiet for a moment. "I- I don't know if I can. What if they catch us? I don't want to die."

"You'll die here if you don't try. How I see it, either way, we may die. But I want to die trying. I won't forgive myself if I don't try."

"I can't die, Grace. I have to take care of my family and our farm. They are counting on me to come back. I'm supposed to marry soon."

"I need to get back to my plantation too. But I can't do anything back home while I'm stuck here, can I?"

My pep talk isn't working. And it is about to be cut short. I need to leave before we are caught together, contemplating a scheme.

"Maybe when Henry has us together, like in bed. That could be our chance. We can catch him off guard. He will be aroused and not thinking straight. One of us can knock him over the head with something heavy. Or we can tie him up."

"Are you crazy?" Annabel asks.

Am I crazy? *Am I crazy?* Henry and his mother are the crazy ones. The guards and servants are the crazy ones. And now I'm beginning to think that Annabel is another crazy one.

I have no words. I stare at her with my mouth open in shock. I am definitely not getting through to her. Great, another lost cause. The only one who cares about all this is Charles. And he isn't here.

"Just think about what I'm saying. Please? When the time comes, we need to work together."

She doesn't reply. Worse, she doesn't agree with me. I leave her room and proceed down the hall to my own.

What do I do now?

CHAPTER 20

I LAY ON MY BED REPLAYING THE CONVERSATION WITH ANNABEL moments ago. I feel more exhausted in this house than I did in my cell underground. Annabel thinks she is helpless to change her future. Yet she talks about returning home. I don't understand. I don't have time to wait for Annabel to come around, if she ever will.

A knock on the door interrupts my thoughts.

"Miss Grace, M'ster Henry's expectin' ya downstairs," Hanna says quietly.

Oh no! Does he know I spoke with Annabel? "Did he say what for?"

"No, miss."

"Okay, tell him I'll be right down."

"M'ster Henry doesn' like ta wait. Imma 'fraid ya need ta come now, chil'."

Shit.

I climb off the bed and follow Hanna down the hallway. Annabel's door is closed. "Is Annabel coming, too?"

"Imma no' sure. I was only tol' ta come get ya."

We travel down the staircase, walk across the house, and pass the dining hall and the parlor. Usually I meet someone in one of those two rooms. Where are we going?

Hanna stops in front of two big doors. She starts to open one before turning to me. "Go on, chil'."

I see the picturesque scene before me—the long gravel road adorned with oak trees that line either side. As I step out, I'm breathless. *Freedom.* I slowly walk through the doorway of the main doors to the front of the house. *Am I about to leave here? Is Hanna helping me escape?*

I look out in front of me, down the curved steps, and see a horse-drawn coach in the circular pathway. Time slows. For a moment, I think back to the day I was brought here with my hands and ankles tied together. Now, I stand here in the same scene, but this time, I find freedom, instead of a nightmare.

My feet take one stair at a time. My mind spins on this new reality. I feel the weight lift off of my body as I descend. All the stress and anxiety inside of me evaporates into thin air. By the time I reach the bottom step, I float like the clouds in the sky.

I approach the coach, and the door swings open. "You took long enough. Get in, or I'll be late."

No! Why is Henry in the coach? I'm supposed to escape *from* him, not actually be *with* him! I can't breathe. I don't move.

"Hurry the fuck up, Grace. I haven't got all day."

What is happening? I climb into the coach because I don't know what else to do. I can't run because he will just chase after me. I sit across from him and stare blankly at his face. What is he doing here?

"Why are you acting so surprised to see me? Didn't Hanna tell you that you were to come meet me?"

"Y-yes." I stutter. I remember Hanna mentioning Henry waiting for me, but when I saw the coach, my mind completely adopted another fantasy. I thought Hanna was helping me escape, just like I asked. I peer out the carriage window as we move away from the house. "Where are we going?"

"Into town. I have a business meeting."

"Why are you taking me?"

"Would you rather stay back at the house? I can tell Hanna to lock you back into your room again, if you'd like."

Hell no. At least I don't think so. I wonder if his business meeting has anything to do with me performing certain activities with him or other people... or both. God, I hope not.

"Where's Annabel?"

He chuckles softly under his breath. "Annabel is currently not in good spirits. And I simply enjoy your company. I figure having you with me will pass the time more quickly. Our journey into town is about an hour and a half long. As for my business meeting later, it is strictly business. I am not into sharing, especially with other men. So you can relax about that matter."

My whole body relaxes. I wonder what his business meeting is about. "Will I be present during the business meeting?"

"Absolutely not. Women cannot participate in such matters. Plus, you would be too much of a distraction. I'm afraid the conversations that take place will not be efficient if you were to accompany me."

"Your mother seems to be involved."

"What my mother and I know does not concern you. Don't push me, Grace," he warns.

"I think your wrong." I'm trapped in this coach with him. If he wants to kick me out, then I'll gladly open the door myself.

He stares at me with narrowed eyes.

"Those papers in the secret cottage that you found me in. They contain information."

Henry leans forward, placing his elbows on his knees. "What did you see?"

Now it's my turn to hold an evil stare back at him. I can't tell him what I know, not yet. I need more information first. The air is thick with unspoken threats.

Just as I think we won't talk the rest of the way into town, Henry says, "Get on your knees."

"Excuse me?"

"Why do you always make me repeat myself. Get. On. Your. Knees."

I lower onto my knees right in front of him. Henry spreads his legs to accommodate the tight space. He slowly unbuttons his trousers.

"Suck."

A small, shabby sign tells me that we arrive in McComb, Mississippi shortly after I satisfy Henry. I never had a penis in my mouth before. Henry was too big to fit all at once. He tried, forcefully, which caused tears to stream down my face. As he jerked my head down harder and harder, I lost my ability to breath. Before I could shove myself off of him, he let all of his fluids into my throat, causing me to further gag.

"Swallow," he demanded.

After he finished, he tidied himself. I sat back on my side of the coach, silently. I was so disgusted with myself and him that I didn't want to talk anymore. I couldn't even bring myself to look at him so I decided to look out the window. I hate him. I even hate myself right now.

We arrive at a discreet, narrow brick building in the heart of the town. Henry steps down from the coach.

"You stay in here. I won't be long."

He locks the door from the outside and enters the undisclosed building. There is no sign in front of this place, which heightens my suspicions further. Henry is definitely involved with murky business. This sour pit in my gut has built a permanent residence.

I gaze out the other window of the coach to the outside world. Other coaches pass by the beautiful trees and flowers along the streets, and people exchange pleasantries and laughter. A church steeple sits on the horizon.

I sigh. Watching the outside life is depressing. This longing starts to physically hurt my chest. I need to calm down and shed some of my gloom. Locked in this coach, there is not much I can do anyway. I tell myself to count and control my breathing so I don't begin to panic.

One…Everything is going to be okay. Two…I'm alive today. Three…I'm not being beaten or tortured. Four—

CHOO CHOO! *Is that a train whistle?* Is there a station nearby? *CHOO CHOO!*

I look out the window to see what direction the train is coming from. Damn it, I can't see anything. I can only hear it. It's loud enough to be close by, though. Where is it coming from? Better yet, where is it going? Is it a passenger train? Who the hell cares. I'll figure out how to get on it regardless.

I startle when the coach door jiggles. Henry climbs in and sits down quietly. He seems to be in a better mood than before. I assume the meeting went well, at least for Henry.

"Did you miss me?"

Nauseating. However, I need to hide my true feelings so he doesn't become suspicious of my fantasy of leaving this place. "Does it look like I missed you?"

"I would say that you look lonely."

"What makes you think that?"

"The way you were looking out the window when I returned."

He really does pay attention. I need to be careful. "I miss living in the outside world, laughing and talking with others." I swallow the lump that forms in my throat. "I miss my parents."

We both sit quietly in the wake of my assertion.

Then, Henry asks, "Were you close to them?"

His question surprises me. "Very." I fight back tears.

We endure another long, awkward silence before he continues, "It was hard on me when I lost my father over thirteen years ago."

I'm afraid to even breathe that he will stop talking. The more information he shares, the more he trusts me. Maybe, just maybe, I can use that to my advantage one day. My eyes plead for him to continue.

Henry intently stares at the floor of the coach. "I don't think my mother cared as much as I did. She fell in love with his money and power. I can't blame her because I'm in love with those things just as much as she is. But my father loved me with all his heart. I know he did."

"How did he die?"

He looks up at me then. "He shot himself."

I gasp and throw my hands over my mouth. "I- I'm sorry. I didn't mean to—"

"Don't apologize. He was a coward."

I feel dizzy from verbal whiplash. One minute, he loves his dad, and the next, he calls him a coward.

Sensing my confusion, Henry explains, "My father, because he was a rich man, took risks—different business ventures, investments, and gambling. He liked a fast lifestyle. Many people loved him, especially his fair share of women. But he also had many who despised him, especially the ones he owed money. You don't want to get mixed up with those people. I guess he finally reached a point where he couldn't handle it anymore. He didn't want any more responsibility.

"Where I found you, in what you call the secret cottage, that was where my father kept all of his misfortunate dealings, from my mother and me. That was where I found his body, after he shot himself. I was nearly eighteen at the time so I could not fully comprehend what mess my father made and what he was really up to.

"He always disappeared after dinner for long periods of time. Sometimes he wouldn't come back home until the next day. So, I decided to follow him one evening. But I was too late. After I discovered his body, I decided to bury him out in the woods, where he belonged, with all of his secrets."

That explains the tombstone Charles and I discovered.

"Wow, I don't know what to say."

"I don't expect you to say anything."

The earlier silence is nothing compared to his recent confession. He spoke about his family with a swiftness that almost made me believe he is comfortable talking about it with me.

I respond to his candidness by simply saying, "You look like him. In the photograph, in the secret cottage, I saw you, your father, and your mother together. You look just like your father. Actually, when you opened the door, and I saw your face for the first time, I didn't know if you were the man in the photograph or the teenage boy."

"Everyone used to tell us that we looked like twins. It used to make my father happy. He was so full of himself. He loved having a son to pass on his legacy. Little did I know what that entailed at the time."

"I'm sure you were proud to be his son," I countered.

"Once upon a time, I guess. After he died, my mother made sure to let me know that I was the new man of the house. The responsibility landed on our shoulders now."

"So your mother forced you at that young age to carry the burden of your father's misfortunes?"

"No, she and I are in this together. We both carry his burdens. We are family, and family comes before all else."

"Well, she's a bitch."

Henry laughs. "She may come across as one to you. But she's taken care of me my entire life. I have much to thank her for. I couldn't have gotten this far without her."

"So you and your mother are left to pay back you father's debts?"

"I guess you can say that."

"Are they paid?"

"Mostly. There are a few loose ends still left to deal with."

"Is that what the business meeting was about?"

"You ask too many questions, you know that?"

I think for a moment before I ask my next question. Do I really want to know the answer. "Am I a loose end?"

"It's complicated."

Wow. I *am* involved with a bigger plan here. He didn't confirm or deny it. Before he shuts me out completely, I want to know one more piece of information. "Did I hear a train earlier?"

"Yes. The train passes through McComb."

I try to stifle my excitement from showing on my face. "Where does it go to?"

"Chicago." Henry gazes out the window. He appears deep into his thoughts, more than likely about his father.

I don't think he realizes that he answered my question. He gave me more information than I expected, and I'm grateful for it. Now, I just need to figure out how to get back to McComb and walk around freely.

"I've never been to Chicago. To be honest, I've never been out of Louisiana."

"That's too bad. You're missing out."

"I guess I don't know what I am missing anyway. So it's no big deal."

"I beg to differ."

"I mean, now I can say I've been to McComb. Too bad I had to stay in the coach. Maybe next time, you will let me out so I can breathe a little fresh air."

"Very funny. We will see about that, if there even is a next time."

CHAPTER
21

O^{N THE WAY BACK, I NOTICE ANOTHER SIGN COMMUNICATING} some direction as to where I'm being held captive—just outside of Kentwood, Louisiana. I realize that I am a far ways from home.

Henry and I arrive back at the house just in time for a late dinner.

"Will your mother be joining us for dinner, tonight?" I ask as we walk through the front doors.

"Actually, no. I have other plans for dinner."

Thank god. I don't want his mother to ruin what turned out to be a somewhat pleasant day. We walk down the hallway in silence. I continue to stay by his side, unsure where I should go without his direction.

Then, Henry takes my hand, causing us to stop. "Thank you for accompanying me to McComb."

"Y-your welcome." His ice blue eyes pierce my soul, an unsettling feeling.

His good looks and charm don't sway me from knowing what really lies beneath his surface. He is unforgiving and cruel, just like his mother. They don't give a damn about people. Henry said so himself. They love money and power.

I have to play along if I'm going to fulfill my goals. I look back into Henry's direct stare with my stormy blue ones.

He lifts his hand to cup my cheek. I despise his touch, but I don't push it away. I can't. He drops his head closer to mine like he might kiss me. I force myself not to move or turn away. He's so close I could simply tilt my head slightly and our lips will touch.

I don't move. I barely breathe.

"Go to your room. Undress. Be naked on the bed and ready in ten minutes."

He teases me. He knows I'm his puppet. *Bastard.*

He drops his hand and smirks. Then, I watch him disappear down another corridor before releasing my breath.

I want to scream at the top of my lungs. I hate his demands. I am a whore now, his plaything. I need to be alone, which is ironic considering I was alone for over a week in that hole. I wanted nothing more than to get out. Now that I'm out, I want to be locked up by myself, where no one can touch me.

Maybe that's what I need to do. I decide on my next plan.

I walk upstairs into my bedroom and close the door. I stare at myself in the mirror. I give myself a good look, eyeing the woman staring back at me with lust. I slowly take off my dress, gently touching my body as I do. I want to feel every touch for myself, knowing that I am the only one who can control me. I glide my hands under my chin, down my neck, and across my collar bone.

The tiny hairs on my arm stand up, and I softly graze my fingertips over my shoulder. I hover across my chest. Along the way, I feel the fullness of my breasts and pinch each nipple.

My dress falls to the floor, and I remove my undergarments and shoes. As I lay on the bed, sprawled out for myself, I continue touching my body. I resume where I just left off and slide my hands from my breasts down my belly to my inner thighs. I imagine Charles. I can't help but picture him as I touch myself.

I imagine him licking me everywhere that I touch. I make my way to my clit and rub my finger back and forth, just as Henry directed me in recent past. The slickness between my folds turns me on more as I stick a finger inside myself, wondering what I feel like.

I pull out and continue to touch my clit in circles this time. My inner core builds a wave of pleasure that I now know I cannot stop. I start to tremble. I'm about to burst into a million pieces from the inside out. I rub faster and faster.

"Oh my god," I cry as I climax.

My body explodes, and I scream. A rush of liquid bursts through my body, soaking my fingers. As I slowly come off my high and work my way down, I smile to myself.

God that felt good. *That* was for me.

Henry walks through the door a few minutes later, seeing me sprawled out on the bed. I couldn't move after the pleasure I gave myself so I decided to stay relaxed here. I still stroke my stomach and my breasts with my fingertips. I like feeling my skin. My breath is still a bit ragged.

"Did you start without me?" Henry asks with a warning tone.

"Maybe," I reply with a sheepish grin, half breathless. I'm not sure if he's angry or if it turns him on. Either way, I don't care.

"You've been a bad girl today." He starts to undress.

What? I have been?

"You stole my plate at lunch today…"

Really? I snicker.

"You made me wait for you to accompany me to my meeting today."

"You're crazy." I can't keep quiet about his ridiculous comments.

"Then, somehow, you get me to open up about my father."

"That wasn't my fault."

"We've essentially skipped dinner because I need to have you, only to find that you've already pleasured yourself without my permission."

Thus, the point of my decision. "I told you that no one can control me."

"And I told you that you're wrong. This deserves a punishment."

Worth it.

Henry leaves the room, almost fully naked. Is he going to whip me with something? I hope not. My back is still recovering from Larsen's previous beating. Henry returns moments later, with Annabel. She is fully clothed and looks like he just woke her from a slumber. Her puffy eyes indicate she has been crying again.

Her eyes bulge, seeing me naked on my bed. We stare at each other in disbelief.

"Grace, you are not allowed to come tonight since you have already done so without my permission. Annabel, strip and get on the bed."

That night was one of the longest nights of my life. Just when I thought it would end, Henry made Annabel and I perform repulsive sexual acts on each other. Sometimes Henry joined in as well. He took pleasure in my disgust. His punishment worked.

The most disturbing part was when Henry sheathed his manhood with a condom before having sex with us, mainly with Annabel. He barely touched me. Seeing him worship her in front of me almost made me threw up, multiple times. I shouldn't care, but watching two people have sex and then being their sloppy seconds is repulsive.

Henry even warned me, "If you get sick on these sheets or us, I swear to God you are going back underground."

I fucking hate him.

I despise him for what he's done to me, Annabel, everyone else here, and our families back home. Unfortunately, there were no weapons in the room I could use. Even if there were, I never had time. He always made sure Annabel had her hands on me.

Now, with everyone gone, my mind races. I don't recall Henry using a condom with me the other night.

Damn him.

I didn't even think about protection. But since he just used one, well more than one, I begin to wonder why he didn't before. Was it intentional? Or did he accidently forget?

I hope I don't get pregnant, especially not with *his* baby. His whole family is fucked up. I would be his prisoner forever.

I need to calm down. I can't think like that. What's done is done. So there is no need to panic, right? *Right?*

I need to speak to Henry about this. Maybe he doesn't realize he forgot to use a condom with me. I need to warn him.

I am due to bleed soon so I guess in a short time, I will find out, I think. The last time I bled was a week before Will and Larsen took me. Or two weeks before? Shit, I don't remember. I never needed to remember, before now.

Henry and I need to talk.

CHAPTER 22

The next morning, Hanna retrieves me from my room, stating that Henry summoned me for brunch on the back patio. As the weeks in October pass by, the weather cooled, making it bearable to enjoy the southern heat, even during the day.

Hanna helps me into a white, lace dress. With capped sleeves, it falls past my knees. I look elegant and poised as I stare in the mirror. Inside, I feel anything but.

Hanna fixes my hair, styled to make sure I won't get hot. When I am presentable, I walk outside. The gentle wind in the air seems to rejuvenate everyone's souls, even the servants, except mine.

I hate this place. I hate Henry.

I take in the scenery. The endless number of leaves have fallen, causing the woods to appear more bare since the last time I was there. The secrets that reside in the forest want to be revealed—the prisoners, Charles, *the fucking game*. The guards line the woods, just like I remember, although it seems like a lifetime has passed. So much has happened since then.

In the gazebo, the brunch table is set for us. However, as I approach the gazebo, I notice the table is set for a party of four. *Who will be joining us?*

I take my seat first, with my back to the woods, while I have the chance. I can't bear the many thoughts of Charles and the other prisoners scouring the woods for survival as I eat like a queen.

I am such a traitor.

Just as I take my seat, I look up and see Henry and Annabel, who is dressed in almost the same outfit, in another form of white lace. I think her puffy eyes will permanently stay that way.

"Good morning, " Henry chirps. A hard stare is my only response, and he chuckles.

Henry sits to the left of me while Annabel picks the seat to my right. "You know, when you summon me down for brunch, I expect to eat with a fork and a knife with my meals. A spoon will not always suffice." I start the meal with my sassiness. It's only going to get worse from here anyway.

"I figure as much. However, I don't trust you," he points to Annabel, "or *you* with a fork or a knife at the moment," he concludes, pointing at me next.

"I'm sure we've proven to you that we have no intention of killing you. We've had some opportunities already. I don't think we've disappointed you yet," I retort.

"It's not my life I worry about. You might take your own lives, and I'm not ready for y'all to die just yet. There is more to come, like last night."

He grins like the devil. *Bastard.* I honestly hated last night. I would welcome an actual beating again than forced to perform sexual acts on Annabel once more, all while Henry watches.

Annabel stays silent. She doesn't even move. She keeps her eyes cast down at the table in front of her.

"You haven't started without me yet, have you, Henry?" The shrill voice sends pins and needles all through my body. Mrs. Edith steps onto the patio with a broad smile. She's in a good mood. *Odd.*

"No, Mother, we haven't."

"Oh, good. I didn't want to miss the show."

"The show?" I ask.

Henry's mother responds first, bursting with excitement to spoil the surprise. "Yes, the show today involves the last remaining prisoners battling to the death."

The blood drains from my face, and I feel faint. *Charles.* "How many remain?"

"Four—all male—which I knew would happen."

Bitch.

"You're wrong," I reply, swallowing my blinding anger.

"How am I wrong? They are about to bring out the remaining four. They all look like men to me."

"You must be forgetting Annabel and I." I look her straight in the eyes.

"Yes, well, soon enough that won't be the case either, I'm sure."

"Mother," Henry warns.

"I'm surprised you haven't gotten bored of your whores yet anyway. That's unlike you, Henry," his mother chastises.

I ignore her snide comments and continue, "I'm confused. If there is a game to the death today, then what was point of finding the orange flag?"

"There is no game about the orange flag." Henry states dryly while adjusting his napkin in his lap.

"Can you please elaborate?" I ask as my voice slides into a higher pitch. My suspicions this whole time were correct. However, hearing the words from Henry's mouth does not make me feel any better. I did not achieve sweet victory with this one. There is no winner here.

"There needed to be a game of some sort to keep y'all motivated to live. Otherwise, it would be too easy."

"I don't know why it couldn't be simple, Henry." His mother chimes in with disappointment. "You always make things too complicated when it doesn't have to be."

"Make what easy?" I look back and forth between them.

Neither of them speaks for a minute as the tension in my belly swells. Then, Henry breaks the ice. Actually, he creates more of it. "Killing all of you," Henry answers, steady and cold, as he looks at me with his glacier eyes.

I shiver at his response. They are psychotic. I'm disposable. I knew I was disposable when I arrived here, but I thought he grew to like my presence at least. I was given more time. I was trying to use that to my advantage. But now I see, there is no advantage. We really are going to die here. There is no out.

"Here they come!" His mother squeals with delight, pulling me away from my depressing thoughts.

I turn in my seat, and the four prisoners are escorted closer to the patio. Their hands are tied with rope, just like I remember.

Then, I see him. *Charles.*

His shoulders slump. He looks defeated. He's been beaten and hasn't seen me in days. He probably thinks I'm dead. But I'm not. I'm right here, dressed up, eating gourmet food, sitting with the enemy. And I can't do a goddamn thing about it.

I am a traitor. And a harlot. But Charles doesn't know that, not yet. It would kill him if he found out.

Our food is brought out to us, but there is no way I can eat. Feeding myself, knowing Charles and the others are starving, is repulsive. Annabel, on the other hand, eats like there is no tomorrow. The way Henry's mother talks, there may not be.

I turn back toward Charles, and his face lifts. He sees me.

Shit.

He raises his hands to shade his eyes from the sun. Yes, it's me, the traitor. Here I am. God, I hate myself now and how this looks to Charles.

The guards gather the four men in a row and untie their wrists. Then more guards appear out of nowhere and form a confining circle around the prisoners.

I can barely hear the main guard telling the prisoners their final directions. All I can make out are short phrases like "—fight to the death—," "—choice of weapon—," and finally "—last one standing."

From the side, two guards carry a long tray with four weapons: a sword, a spear, an axe, and a dagger. I can't believe this is really happening. I don't know if I can watch. I grab at my stomach as increasing panic twists it in pain.

"It appears, Henry, that one of your whores is affected greatly by this battle. I wonder if she is concerned for the one who took her place days ago."

Henry studies my face. God, I hate that woman. She isn't wrong. She's in fact dead on the money. I need to be careful. But how can I watch three of these men die. Even if I don't look, I will hear it anyway. There is no way around this.

Annabel's face is also stricken with horror. Already on the verge of tears, her hands cover her mouth, and she quietly begins to sob.

I must save myself, "I don't know what you are talking about. I've seen my mother and father murdered in front of me. It doesn't matter to me who dies out here. I have no love left in my body to care anymore."

Henry and his mother still aren't satisfied.

"So you see, how can I care about anyone? I think you should just kill them all and get it over with." I can't believe I just said that out loud. My heart hurts trying to keep up the façade.

Both of them glance back at the brawl. I follow their lead. Annabel continues to show her emotions. Maybe they know she's a lost cause.

The table of weapons passes the prisoners, and one by one, each man selects their weapon of choice. Charles is the last to pick, so he receives the dagger—the weapon no one wants. It has neither power nor length to do much of anything.

Now I really don't want to watch.

As he is forced to grab his weapon, Charles looks up at me and raises his dagger toward our table. I think I'm going to be sick. I act like I didn't notice his gesture. The world blurs and eventually fades away as I fix my stare straight ahead.

The main guard announces, "Fight!"

All four prisoners jockey in place to prepare their ready stance for battle. They stand in a small circle of their own with all their weapons drawn.

Charles looks out of place since his weapon appears to be the least effective. He needs the shortest distance to strike someone. A miracle will honestly be the only thing to save him. To his right, the prisoner holds the sword. To his left, the prisoner wields the axe. The prisoner with the spear stands directly in front of him.

The prisoner with the sword strikes first, toward Charles, who immediately steps back and swings his dagger to block the potential hit.

I stifle a gasp and want throw my hands over my face to cover my eyes. But I stay stoic.

"Oh, so close!" Mrs. Edith shouts. "That's too bad."

I burn with fury. The other two prisoners split off and begin to attack each other in their own battle. My eyes lock on Charles, and I say a silent prayer. *Please don't die.*

Charles continues to defend himself against the sword. The spear lunges toward the axe who dodges the spear and swings around, causing the spear to break into two parts. The head of the spear drops to the ground, and the prisoner now timidly holds half of his stick in his hands.

Noticing a vulnerable situation, the prisoner fighting Charles turns his attention for a moment to the now doomed prisoner and swipes at him. With little to defend himself, the ill-fated prisoner holds his lowly stick at the sword, but it only splinters further. The sword slices the prisoner's torso.

"Ahhh!!!" The prisoner yells and falls, wincing in pain.

The prisoner with the axe throws his weapon down hard on the condemned prisoner from behind. One prisoner down, two more to go. God this is brutal.

Charles lunges at the prisoner still holding the sword and stabs him in the side. But it appears to only graze him, anger him. He swings violently multiple times at Charles, who dodges the sword by moving out of the way or defending himself with the help of his dagger.

Then, the man with the axe joins the prisoner attacking Charles. *Shit, two against one.*

"Say goodbye to your boyfriend," Mrs. Edith says.

She doesn't know Charles like I do. I have seen him in action. He has no problem killing a man. He can be ruthless.

Henry sets his napkin on the table, stands, and walks to the edge of the gazebo for a closer look. Perhaps he can't abide his mother's comments either.

The prisoner with the axe swings at Charles just as the other continues to thrust his sword. Charles tucks and rolls between the two. He races over to the fallen spear head and throws it at the chest of the prisoner who holds the sword.

He doesn't see it coming. The impact of the spear collides with his heart and he crumbles to the ground, grabbing the spear from his chest. Blood gushes from his body. Another prisoner is finished. Two down, one to go.

The prisoner with the axe stumbles, discovering Charles's capabilities. He holds his axe in the ready position to strike. Charles stalks over to him without hesitation with only the dagger in his hand.

Charles is the hunter. The man with the axe is the prey.

The prisoner takes an apathetic swing at Charles as he gets closer. Charles easily dodges the attack by side stepping. Then Charles grabs the prisoner's wrist that holds the axe and shoves the dagger into his stomach. Charles holds it there, twisting it for good measure. Then, he rips it out, and the prisoner falls as well.

Holy shit!

Charles is the last man standing. Relief and pure happiness fill my heart. However, my happiness is immediately replaced by guilt. He had to kill other men to survive, all in front of me, who he thought was most likely dead.

He drops his dagger and looks up toward the gazebo. Henry motions with a raised hand to bring the surviving prisoner over to us.

My heart pounds in my ears as Charles gets closer.

"Congratulations," Henry slowly claps when Charles approaches our table. Four guards flank him. Charles stares at me. In a flash, I see his pain, his love, his confusion. I look at him with sorrowful eyes of apology. *I'm sorry for sitting here with the devil while watching you fend for your life.*

Henry disrupts our quiet moment. "You put on quite a show out there."

Charles pries his eyes away from mine to look at the person responsible for all this. His green eyes change from love to anger in a spilt second. "Is that what you call this? A show?"

Henry smirks. "What else would I call it?"

Charles balls his fists at his sides, and his mouth thins into a tight, straight line. "Maybe you should call it hell. Maybe you should call it your worst nightmare. Because that is exactly what I've been through, what we all have been through." Charles gestures to Annabel and I with his last statement.

"Grace and Annabel appear to be doing just fine. Look how relaxed and well fed they are. I'm sure they would tell you of the pleasures they've endured since staying in the house. Wouldn't you say, Grace? Tell him how much pleasure I have given you two over the last few days."

There is in fact no pleasure endured at all. However, I can't deny Henry, or he may kill me. I glance at Charles, hoping he knows that none of this is true.

"I can't seem to get enough sleep anymore around here with all the noise you two make," Henry's mother connivingly states at the most inconvenient time.

That little witch!

Charles stares at me with now lifeless eyes, the green in them that I love so much fades, even as his body still contains wrath. We are being tested. We are being manipulated into showing our true feelings.

I can't let that happen. I need to shut it off. And that's exactly what I do. I look back at Charles with my own lifeless eyes.

Charles finally declares with passion, "It doesn't matter because I won. I beat this game. I'm the smartest and the strongest here. Now that I've won, you need to let me go."

A few seconds pass by of silence before Henry and his mother combust in deeply sinister laughter.

"There is no winner here. Don't you get that? There is no game to be won. Games like this are only meant to be played. You are the player. I am the master of ceremony. I say when it's over. I say when you lose and when you win. And unfortunately for you, you lose."

Henry pulls a pistol from behind his back and aims right at Charles. I watch in slow motion as Charles shifts his eyes toward me.

I can't show any emotion. I scream on the inside. Henry pulls the trigger, and the shot blasts in my ear, in my heart. I turn straight ahead toward Henry's mother, who watches me, waiting for a sign.

Don't look. Don't cry. No emotion.

I look down at my food and begin to eat.

My love, I'm sorry.

CHAPTER
23

CHARLES COLLAPSES, AND HIS BLOOD POOLS BY OUR FEET. Annabel shrieks in horror and starts to shake.

Henry sits down at the table and sets his pistol, which is still smoking, between him and me.

Mrs. Edith looks between Henry and I with an evil queen smirk on her face.

I want to wipe off that smile by shooting her in the fucking head. My father taught me how to shoot growing up. I have wicked aim. It could be over in a few seconds, just like how Charles's life ended.

But then my life would end at the hands of all these guards and servants. What would have been the point to all of this?

I need to escape. I need to be free. Charles didn't die just for me to die as well, just seconds later. I can't give up.

I pretend to enjoy the food with my stupid spoon. It's difficult to swallow, though, around the bile that demands release.

Mrs. Edith stands from the table and sashays toward the house. *Where the hell is she going?* She must be done since the "show" is over.

Annabel continues to sob. She needs to stop. It's not fair for her to shed tears for the man I love, especially when I can't. I plan to later, when I'm alone for no one to witness my torture.

Henry eats until his plate is clean and uses his napkin to wipe his face. "So tell me, Grace, did you enjoy *that* show?"

I have no words for him. I can only try to channel my sassiness. I take a silent, deep breath in and force myself to say, "I've seen better."

He snorts at my reply. "Then maybe I'll have to show you something better later."

The servants come to carry Charles's lifeless body away. His blood stained the bricks by our table. I can't look over, or I'll start to cry.

Mrs. Edith returns with two glasses of white wine and sets them by Annabel's and my meal settings. She hates us with her whole being so why would she bring us glasses of wine? Aren't there servants for that, anyway?

"I figure you girls need a drink after that show," she states. "Plus, I'd like to make a toast." She gestures all of us to lift our glasses. "To the end of the game!" she happily shouts.

I loathe this monster. I can't toast to that. I watch everyone take a drink from their glasses before I dare to sip mine. Annabel gulps it down.

Mrs. Edith spurs me on, "Drink up, Grace. Relax a little." She pushes me to drink.

I look down at my glass, contemplating. Although I'm trying to keep a front, I can't bring myself to drink it. Something doesn't feel right. She assesses me with sinister eyes. Her wickedness is frightening.

Suddenly, Annabel grabs at her throat, choking. *What the hell?* She starts to foam at the mouth, and her face tints a shade of purple. The blood vessels in her neck turn black. She gags and coughs until her whole body goes limp.

Henry abruptly stands from his chair, knocking it over, "What the fuck?"

Poison.

Mrs. Edith continues to stare at me. I still hold the wine glass in my hand. I want to put it down, but the power it contains makes me hold onto it longer than I should.

"Mother, what have you done?"

She slowly tears her gaze away from mine and looks up at her son. "I did it for you, Henry."

Henry's face fills with concern as he turns to me. "Grace, did you drink it?" he asks with urgency. *Is he worried about me?*

I want him to sweat it out a bit. I want him to feel sadness, just like what I went through. I know it's not much, but hearing him in an ounce of pain rewards for me. It's music to my ears. I stay silent.

He comes closer to me, "Grace, did you drink any of it?"

I look him in the eyes for a moment before giving my answer to his mother. "No." I pour the contents of my glass out on the ground next to me. I thought about shattering it on the very bricks that hold Charles's blood or hurling it at Mrs. Edith's face. But what good would any of that do? I need to keep Henry on my side.

Henry visibly relaxes, and I'm surprised with his comment, "Oh, thank God." He holds onto the table for support and hangs his head in relief.

"Mother, why the fuck would you do this?"

"I told you, I'm doing this for you. You are too distracted. You are losing sight of what we are trying to accomplish. We need them gone—all of them! Not one single heir is supposed to be alive! Those were the requirements."

Heir?

She continues, "Did you forget the stipulations? We need to control the crops and have access to distribute them by train and maritime. We cannot do that if there are survivors. All traces of family need to be annihilated so no one lays claim to inherit what was left behind. This is necessary to pay back your father's debts. And we will be left with ultimate control and more money than God himself could ever wish for!"

Her tone becomes more portentous. "The debt collectors from your father's senseless business dealings will come back for us if we do not satisfy the terms. Don't take their threats lightly. You need to do what is best for us—you and me. No one else."

All of the puzzle pieces click together in my mind. The papers documented many small farmers in the southern region, but only a small group of us have larger plantations. Charles told me his family were rice farmers. Another prisoner had tobacco. My family grew strawberries. Other plantations contain indigo, crawfish, sugar cane, cotton, and figs. The list goes on.

Holy hell, they could potentially own the entire southeastern region if they really captured all of us! They will have a monopoly on everything. All the debt they owe back from his father would be easily paid off and more.

Mrs. Edith continues, "But now, you've decided to play you own game with these whores, and you are getting soft on me. I had to end it for you because you won't."

"I am not a whore!" I rush to my feet. "You think I'm weak. You may think I'm innocent. But I'm not. And if I was a whore, then you've been outsmarted by one. How does that make you feel?" I throw my napkin down and storm off.

My ears ring with a god-awful noise, the gunfire right by my ear that killed the only person left worth fighting for. I walk around the side of the house. I need fresh air, away from the dead bodies and blood. Adrenaline runs through my veins.

Henry and his mother will potentially control the entire southeastern part of the country. They will be unstoppable. What's next? Politics? Infiltrating the government? That can't happen. This country would become an awful place, run by awful people.

"Grace! Wait!"

I spin around and see Henry chasing after me. I look past him to see if his mother follows. Luckily, it's just Henry.

"Where are you going?" he asks.

"Where am I going? Where can I go? I am held captive here." I throw my hands up in the air.

"I want you here," he states calmly.

His confession floors me. Well, he has a twisted way of showing it. I thought I was just a game to him, too.

"Well, your mother clearly doesn't want me here. She just tried to kill me! And she would have succeeded if I had let my guard down."

"That's why I like you."

"You like me?" I sound like a parrot, asking for him to repeat himself.

"Yes. You are constantly aware of your surroundings and how to act when appropriate in different situations. You can adapt. You've seen death, but you continue to live. That's admirable."

He's not wrong. But I survive for my escape and now for the cause of their deaths. Revenge will be sweet.

"Your mother..." I consider my next words carefully.

"What about my mother?"

"She doesn't like me. She wants to get rid of me. I am not safe here anymore. For all I know, she will kill me in my sleep tonight."

Henry doesn't even blink an eye before saying, "Then you will sleep with me tonight."

"What?"

"Yes, that way I will make sure she doesn't hurt you."

Is Henry falling in love with me? Henry is incapable of love, but maybe I can gain his trust. If he trusts me, then maybe I can turn him against his mother, eventually. I want leave as soon as possible. But my plan may take a while longer.

My family's plantation is all that I have left now. It's been abandoned for weeks. Hopefully someone there still manages the crops. I want to go back.

"What will you do when your mother is gone?" I ask Henry.

"What do you mean when she is gone?"

"Dead, no longer able to be with you. When it's just yourself to take care of everyone else's property and crops. Who will help you?"

Henry looks down at the floor. "I guess I haven't thought about that. She's been with me this entire time throughout this plan."

"You need someone who will help you in the long term, to be your partner. You need to be able to trust that person. Because what y'all are pulling off is a mega-operation. You will be too vulnerable if it's just you alone left to manage it by yourself. More than likely, you will have more people try and take all this land back, possibly from any surviving families who owned it before, or maybe even from the people that your father owed."

Henry quietly processes my words, intently listening.

"All I'm saying is to be careful with whom you trust. Look for someone who will always be at your side. Your mother won't be with you forever."

"So are you trying to convince me that person is you?"

I stare at him a few moments, like I'm thinking it over, when in fact I already know my answer. I quietly relish my triumph. "I've seen behind the scenes what you've done to get to this point. I survived those things. I'm still here. For all the lives that have been lost over this project and for all the pain I endured, I want to see it finished and carried out appropriately."

He doesn't say a word after my speech. He simply takes my hand and walks me back inside. I decide to not to speak anymore either. I need to give him time. Now, I have time on my side.

CHAPTER 24

Two days pass after that conversation Henry and I had on the side of the house. He kept his word, and I slept with him to make sure his mother wasn't going to kill me in the middle of the night. Of course, having me in his bed conveniently allowed him to have me in more ways than one.

If I could have found a way to kill Henry while he slept, I would have done it already. I still don't have access to sharp objects or anything of concern for their lives or mine. I am settling for the right time to seek my revenge, but I fall short on the logistics.

I'm watched like a hawk, although Henry trusts me a little more than when this whole charade started. He treats me more like his partner than his prisoner.

However, the last two nights proved difficult for me to fall asleep. I replay those horrible events of watching Charles fight for his life only for his life to abruptly end. I also lay awake thinking about my parents, Annabel, and the other prisoners.

I finally start to relax when I picture Mrs. Edith and Henry's lifeless bodies right before my eyes. I make sure that is the last image before I drift into a peaceful slumber.

After the second night, I wake up to a loud noise in the hallway. *What time is it?* I must have slept in because there is a tray of breakfast for me next to the bed. A note lays next to the tray:

A last-minute meeting came up that I could not miss. I decided to leave you sleeping and ordered Hanna to bring you breakfast in bed. I won't be long. - H

I'm thankful for the extra rest. Between my recurring nightmares and Henry's commands in the bedroom, I am exhausted.

Bang! Bang! Bang!

What is that commotion in the hallway? Sounds like someone kicking down a door.

I climb off the bed, put my nightgown back on, and walk to the door. I turn the handle and find it unlocked. I hesitate before leaving the doorway to make sure this isn't a trap or figment of my imagination. This gesture is just another one of the little ways that Henry makes me feel less like a prisoner and more like his equal.

I slowly open the door and look up and down the hallway. The loud noise stopped, and no one is in sight. *Wait, I'm alone.* I seize this rare opportunity and walk toward the staircase. I peer over the edge of the banister. Still, no one in sight.

I turn back for one last glance. No one is there. I listen carefully for any footsteps. None. I carefully descend the stairs. I reach the bottom and let out a sigh of relief. Silly how these small accomplishments feel like such a big deal now.

I cautiously turn the corner, thinking surely a servant or two are nearby, but I don't encounter anyone else. My heart beats louder now. Could this actually be happening? Can I make it out the door before anyone notices? I can hide outside until the coast is clear to steal a horse and ride to McComb. It wasn't that far, from what I remember.

I pass the dining room and the parlor with my sights on the front doors. *Keep your eyes on the prize.* I can taste victory. Freedom. I reach out for the door, with mere steps left.

"There you are." Her voice sounds like nails on a chalkboard. I freeze, and goosebumps rise up and down my arms.

No! I'm so close! I turn around to face the wicked witch.

"Where do you think you're going?"

Fuck her. I don't need to answer her. I choose to stay silent. She takes a step closer to me, but I hold my ground.

"I asked you a question, *whore*, and I expect an answer. Were you trying to escape?"

"Fuck. You."

Mrs. Edith's lips curl up on both sides—the smile of evil before the hunter kills his prey. She draws a knife from behind her back.

Oh God.

For every step she takes forward, I take one back. I'm unarmed. I know better than this.

"I walked into your room to find you, but to my surprise, you weren't in there. When I walked back down the hallway, I saw my son's door was open. I decided to go in and see if you were in there since my son can't seem to let you out of his sight. Again, to my surprise, you weren't, but this was."

She holds up the note that Henry left for me with her other hand.

"Now that I know he's gone, it's just you and me. He can't protect you now, you little bitch."

She dives at me with the knife. I reach my hands up to block her. My back slams into the front doors I was trying to escape through just moments ago.

I struggle as she tries to stab my neck and eventually gain a firm grip on her arms. She slides me against the door so my weight shifts, and we fall to the floor. The sudden impact slams my head onto the ground, and pain from the back of my head radiates all over my skull. I think I even black out for a split second. I lose my grip on her arms on the way down.

Her body is splayed on top of me. I try to push her off of me to create more space to wiggle my way out from underneath her and run. I stretch out my arms, but she is too quick.

"Ahhhh!" I feel a sharp pain on my side from where the knife slices me.

"You are ruining everything!" She sits on top of me, and I can't buck her off. Raising both hands up above her head, she poises with the knife, about to strike again. "You deserve to die!"

I cover my face, just hoping that she stabs me in the chest and lets me bleed out. Put me out of my misery.

BANG!

Oh my God. She shot me?! *Wait, did she have a gun?*

I open my eyes, and Mrs. Edith slumps over on the floor beside me with a fresh gunshot wound in her forehead. Henry holds his pistol forward with smoke still coming out of the barrel.

My mouth hangs open as I try to process how I'm not dead. I didn't think it would come to this. I shift to stand but then wince from the pain in my side.

Fucking bitch. I can't believe she stabbed me.

Henry rushes over, practically shoving his dead mother out of the way to reach me. He curses under his breath. Lifting me into his arms, he carries me to one of the couches in the parlor room.

"I'm going to get blood on your cream couch," I say to him.

"Is that what you care about right now?"

I shrug. I'm sure the couch was expensive. There is no way that the blood stain will come out.

He groans. "You're unbelievable."

"You just shot, and *killed*, your own mother. You're one to talk."

"I had to."

"No, you didn't have to. You could have just let her kill me. Then this whole thing would have finished for good."

"I couldn't let her do that."

"And why not?" I want him to say it. I want to hear him say he wants me. He wants me by his side to help manage his awful plan. I want him to trust me enough, and eventually I'll figure out a way to screw him over in the end. I'll ruin him and his reputation so badly that he wishes he was dead.

"I can't kill the mother of my unborn child."

All the blood rushes out of my head. I forgot. I forgot about not using a condom that first night or the other nights since. I was so preoccupied with staying alive that I forgot my period is due.

"H-how do you know? It's so early to tell," I reply, with a quiver in my voice.

He looks at me so confidently and answers just the same, "Your body is different. I can tell you are with child." He tends to my wound, and I start to tremble inside.

"Why didn't you use a condom with me that first night? Or any other night after?"

"I wanted to plant my seed with a strong woman like you, someone just as powerful as my mother and I. I knew it from the second I watched you take the beating from Larsen. I was angry when that boy took your spot. You could have lasted longer, longer than you gave yourself credit."

Seriously? He admires me because I could have taken more of a lashing? "You are a fucking asshole."

"So you've told me before, in so many ways."

"This has been your plan the entire time I've been inside this house?"

"Yes." He played me while I was playing him. What a pair we are. "Now, I plan to take care of you and our son. Y'all are my new family now. I won't let you two out of my sight."

"A son?"

"Yes, to continue my bloodline and legacy, just like my father did with me. The Sullivan surname and our fortunes will last forever."

I can't breathe. There is no way I'll ever be able to leave. What the hell am I going to do now?

CHAPTER
25

THE NEXT MORNING, HENRY AND I TRAVEL TO McCOMB FOR A doctor's visit to check on my health and the potential baby. Henry wants a doctor to evaluate me as soon as possible. I think Henry is being a little over dramatic because I barely even know if I'm pregnant. He believes he is acting completely rational.

I replay the events from the recent days. How much more can a human being take?

Last night, Henry made me sleep with him again. He had a hard time falling asleep too, probably from the guilt of killing his own mother. *Good riddance.* There was one less crazy person in this world.

I thought about killing Henry in his sleep. I pictured him falling into a deep sleep and then strangling the life out of him. Unfortunately, the wound in my side weakened my strength. And the fact that Henry never really slept brought more of a challenge than I was willing to accept.

So here we are, both exhausted, walking to the doctor's house that resides in the heart of McComb. We knock on the door and wait. My fingers fiddle together.

A butler opens the door and greets us.

"Good morning, we are here to see Dr. Fontenot," Henry explains.

The butler bows. "Follow me, please."

We walk inside the beautiful two-story house. A staircase sits to the left as soon as we walk inside, and we are escorted to the parlor room on the right.

"Please wait in here while I find Dr. Fontenot." The butler bows again and leaves.

Henry sits in the wingback chair, and I plop on the couch. We both stay silent, waiting anxiously to see if I'm really pregnant. Henry hopes that I am. I pray that I'm not.

An older gentleman enters the room. "Hello. I'm Dr. Edward Fontenot." He shakes Henry's hand.

"Hello, Dr. Fontenot. Thank you for seeing us on such short notice. I am Henry Sullivan, III, and this is Grace."

I stand and slightly bow my head with the manners my mother taught me from such a young age. Dr. Fontenot stands a few inches shorter than me, with short blonde hair and bright blue eyes. He sports a round tummy and a jolly face. If I didn't know any better, I would think he was Santa Claus's younger brother.

"It is nice to meet you," I say to Dr. Fontenot.

"What can I do for y'all?"

"Grace is with child. I'd like for you to see if you can confirm her pregnancy and check on her overall health."

"How far along do you think you are?" Dr. Fontenot turns to me.

What do I say? There is no way that he can tell I'm pregnant this early. "I'm unsure. I've only barely missed my menstruation maybe within the last few days. But I have also been under a lot of stress."

Henry glares at me. I don't plan to elaborate about my "stresses" to the doctor, but he does need to know that there is a possibility I may not be pregnant.

"What kind of stress?" The doctor's brow furrows with concern. Henry continues to stare daggers at me.

"I fell and cut my side yesterday. Lately, I haven't been wanting to eat. I just have a lot on my mind."

"Oh, I see." The doctor puts his finger up by his mouth. Henry visibly relaxes.

"Sometimes lack of eating can be a sign of early pregnancy," Dr. Fontenot explains. "I need to examine you a little further. Grace, please follow me."

"I'm coming, too." Henry boldly states.

"I don't think that is a good idea. Men are usually not comfortable with how I need to examine their partners." Henry pauses, and the doctor continues, "We will be back in just a few minutes."

Henry nods and concedes.

"This way, Grace."

I follow Dr. Fontenot to a room at the back of the house. There is a long table that he instructs me to lay on. I shiver from the cold surface.

"I need you to lift up your legs and pull down your undergarments." He walks around to the end of the table at my feet.

"Excuse me?"

"I need you to pull down your undergarments and slide down toward me."

No way. I stay exactly where I am.

"I will be brief. I need to examine your lady parts, only for a few moments. The faster you do as I instruct, the faster this will be over."

I reluctantly position as he directed and hold my breath. While the doctor examines me, I take advantage of the situation of being alone with him.

"Is there a train that passes through McComb?" Dr. Fontenot quickly rises up between my legs. "I heard one earlier and was just wondering how often the train comes by. I love hearing the sound it makes when it passes through a town."

He continues his examination as he answers, "Ah, yes. Well, the train doesn't just pass through here. It actually stops to allow passengers on and off twice a day, six in the morning to head south to New Orleans and then again at three in the afternoon to head back north to Chicago."

"If I wanted to hear the train better, how close are we to the station?"

"Not that far. It's by the church, which is just north from here." Before I can speculate how I will return to McComb, alone, the doctor removes his gloves. "Ok, all done here. Pull up your garments, and let's go have a chat with your husband."

The words to correct him are on the tip of my tongue, but I dare not seek Henry's wrath this close to formulating my escape. Dr. Fontenot and I return to the parlor.

"Well, congratulations. It seems like you two are having a baby."

Can this nightmare get any worse? How could he even tell? I can't even tell. Henry's face breaks into a huge smile.

"Grace's cervix and labia appear to be a bluish color and are slightly engorged. The blood flow has increased to her vaginal area, which is a positive indication of bearing a child. She needs to have regular checkups every few months. I can come travel to your home, or you can come back here if you'd like. But she is due for another checkup in three months."

I must control this situation as much as I can. "Since you have meetings here in town, Henry, maybe we can continue to come here. It would be nice to get out of the house once in a while, anyway."

"I think that should be fine. Do we make an appointment for that now, Dr. Fontenot?"

"You can, let me write down the date so I will remember not to take any house calls that day. I'll be right back."

After the doctor leaves the room, I turn to Henry, "By any chance, can we plan on coming in the afternoon? I've heard that pregnancy can make the woman very ill in the mornings. I'd hate to make the journey here longer having to stop every few miles to clear my stomach contents."

"Of course."

"Thank you."

Surprisingly, three months fly by. In fact, I even become sick in the mornings so my excuse for making an afternoon visit was validated. This also confirmed the fact that I am pregnant.

I struggle with the thoughts of having Henry's child. I feel in some way I betrayed Charles, although he isn't here anymore. I know time has passed and I should be over him by now, but I haven't properly mourned his loss. My only chance is whenever I am alone, which is hardly at all.

Memories of me and Charles in the woods together, his green eyes, and his kindness haunt my dreams. He will always have a place in my heart. The way he spoke to me, touched and kissed me, and stood up to the guards and took his beatings to protect me was the only human kindness during my stay here.

Henry is true to his word, though. He constantly cares for me and the baby. If I need anything, within reason, he provides. I have to admit, seeing how passionate he is about me and the baby makes me want to feel like life can be normal.

He doesn't kiss me or grab my hand to dance in the kitchen, like my parents used to do. He doesn't shower me with gifts or let me go into town by myself, not that I expect him to. But he doesn't lay an unwanted hand on me. He doesn't lock me inside any rooms. I'm given clean clothes, sheets, and food at my disposal.

I ask for Hanna from time to time, but Henry tells me she is busy with other tasks for him. Most of the time, Henry brings me my food or anything else I may need. It's hard to tell if he really likes to spend time with me or if this is his way to keep a close eye on me and the baby. Maybe this is his way of making sure no one can potentially harm me, like Will or Larsen.

The other day, I regurgitated so much that I couldn't catch my breath, and I collapsed on the floor in the bathroom. Sharp pains filled my belly, and I hunched over, grabbing my torso. Henry was close by, found me on the bathroom floor, and carried me to bed. He spent the rest of the day applying a wet cloth to my forehead and offering water and food when I could finally hold it down.

Henry massages my feet from time to time, reads to me and the baby randomly, and draws baths for me when I cannot do it myself. These moments allow me to picture what a normal life would be like with Henry.

However, something still doesn't feel right. During these three months, four carriages have arrived and gone around the left side of the house, just like mine did when I was captured. I haven't ventured outside to the hole mainly because I'm a coward. I think it would remind me too much of Charles. I honestly don't want to know the truth. To mentally survive, I need to ignore.

I also do not see Will and Larsen much anymore. Henry doesn't trust them enough to keep their hands off of me. That's the sad truth, but I'm not complaining.

After these three months, my mind waffles on how to proceed. Do I stay and live with what life has now been given to me? Or do I betray Henry and escape to freedom? Will I ever truly escape Henry? Will he come looking for me? Do I plan on keeping his baby when I leave?

I ponder too many questions without answers. When I start to think too hard, I become nauseous all over again. So I tune it out and continue to live each day, at least not worrying if it will be my last.

Before I know it, the day for my visit with Dr. Fontenot is upon me. Henry finds me in the parlor.

"Are you ready?" he asks excitedly. He stands behind me and wraps his arms around my body, placing his hands on my growing belly.

In some twisted way, I like knowing I bring joy to Henry. Everything I have been through originated by greed and hate. Having an ounce of love and desire makes me happy and lifts my spirits, even if it's just for brief moments in time. I look for strength any way I can.

"Before we go, I have a request," I say confidently.

Henry stiffens. "Yes?"

"I'd like Hanna to accompany us today."

He drops his hands from off my belly and paces back and forth. "Absolutely not. There is no reason that she needs to join us. She will be more useful here."

"Actually, I disagree." Henry stares at me in silence, waiting for me to continue. "Last time we went to the doctor's office, you were not allowed to come to the back with me. Do you remember?"

"Yes."

"Well, I was very uncomfortable with the examination Dr. Fontenot performed. Who knows what he will do this time. So I'd like a female presence with me. Hanna's helped me this whole time. So I'd like for her to join me when you cannot."

Henry stands very still, like a statue. I can't gauge his response. Then he speaks, "Okay, I will fetch her. Wait here."

I sit down with my heart beating fast. What if this works?

"Did you plan a meeting today since you're coming back into town?" I ask Henry. Hanna gazes out of the coach window, pretending not to listen to our conversation.

"I did. Any opportunity for meetings to expand my business, I jump on. I hope you don't mind."

"No, not at all. I have Hanna with me today so I won't be bored." I wait a few minutes before adding, "Unless you want to drop Hanna and I off at the doctor's house while you go to your meeting?"

"No, I'd rather wait and see how the doctor's visit goes. Then I plan on taking you two with me to the meeting."

Hanna turns her head toward me. I glance briefly into her eyes and look back to Henry. "That really isn't necessary. It would be a waste of time."

"No time is wasted knowing you and the baby are safe. So drop it."

"What if the baby and I get tired? I'd like to get back as soon as possible and lay down. I'm sure this visit will be unpleasant, just like the last time."

"I sho can take care o' Miss Grace, M'ster Henry."

Hanna's respond surprises me. Does she know? Does Henry know? Can he sense something is off? He looks at Hanna and back at me.

"You see, we will be fine. All you have to do is drop us off and pick us back up. We will be at the doctor's home. I'm sure we will be taken care of there while we wait for you to finish up. It will be much better than waiting in this little coach."

Henry's silent stare narrows. I hold my breath waiting for his reply.

"Fine."

I hold my face still, not to register the shock, amazement, and relief I feel. "Thank you."

The carriage pulls up in front of the doctor's residence. Hanna exits first, and I start to follow. *Can Henry hear my heart beating?*

He tugs my arm, and I turn around. Henry looks at me straight into my eyes. "Let me know if he does anything to hurt you. If so, I'll kill him."

I swallow. "Okay, I will."

"I'll be back as quick as I can."

Then he does something strange. He kisses me, long and hard, on the lips.

What is he doing, and what am I doing? One minute I want to leave, and the next I feel like I need to stay. I climb down the coach to stand next to Hanna and watch Henry disappear down the road.

"Excuse me, madam." The doctor's butler startles me.

"I'm sorry."

"No bother. Please come this way. The doctor is expecting you." The butler ushers us into house and through the entryway to the parlor. "Please wait here while I inform Dr. Fontenot that you are here." The butler bows and walks away.

I immediately reach for Hanna's arm. "Hanna, I need you to do something for me." She's silent, yet her eyes meet mine. My nerves quake inside me. I can't fail now. "I need you to go to the train station and buy me a ticket."

I retrieve cash from the top part of my dress and hand it to her. She tentatively takes it.

"I don't know where the train station exactly is, but it is by the church, north of here. The doctor said it's not far, just down the way a little. This is the part where I need you, please," I plead, with begging eyes. *Please don't let me down.*

"I- I dunno."

"Hanna, please."

Before she can respond, the butler returns. "Dr. Fontenot will see you now. This way."

"I'll be there in one minute. I seem to have forgotten something in the carriage. My servant will retrieve it. She should be back shortly."

"Very well." The butler leaves to give me one last minute of alone time with Hanna.

"Hanna, I'll meet you at the train station. The train leaves around three. As soon as my visit here is done, I'll meet you there. I can't have the train leave without me."

"What'll he do ta me?"

I didn't think about that. Once Henry realizes I'm gone, he will be angry, furious. I can't allow him take out his anger on Hanna. She won't survive. There is only one option.

"Come with me."

"Come wit' ya?"

"Yes, come with me. We can have a fresh start somewhere new." I don't know what possessions Hanna has back at the main house, but I highly doubt she knew she had the ability to leave today. I hope she doesn't have something so important that she feels obligated to stay for. "Do you have everything you need?"

"I dunno."

"Hanna, are you with me?"

I'm at her mercy. All it takes is for her to say yes or no. My fate lies in her hands.

"Imma wit' ya, chil'."

My heart bursts with joy. "Then here, take this." I give her more money, enough to buy two tickets.

Just then, the butler enters the room.

"Can you please show my servant, Hanna, to the front doors. She is going to fetch my carriage for my forgotten item."

"I'm sure Dr. Fontenot can spare his carriage for you if you like."

"No, Hanna doesn't mind the walk. We've been sitting in the carriage for a while now coming here. I think she'll like some fresh air. Wouldn't you agree, Hanna?"

"Yessum, Miss Grace."

"Plus, Henry's business meeting is not that far from here, so he should be back soon."

"As you wish," the butler finally concedes.

Hanna gives me one last look before she follows the butler out of the parlor room toward the front doors.

I sigh, and the doctor walks in. "Good to see you again, Mrs. Sullivan."

My stomach curdles, hearing the doctor call me by that name. Any connection to Henry outside of his estate seems foreign. I am still a prisoner in my own body.

Like before, I don't correct the doctor on his error because there really is no point. Henry has never brought up marriage or asked me to marry him during these last couple of months. His kind gestures from time to time are sweet, but I remind myself that he does them for his unborn child, not for my benefit. I am merely a vessel to carry on his name and heritage to the next generation.

Although Henry is fond of me, I know he does not love me. He is not capable of love. I never let myself believe otherwise. Henry told me himself that he strives for power and money. He wants to pass these vices off to his son one day. He wants to spread his dominance.

There is no room for love and kindness in his dark, infested soul. I thought that maybe, just maybe, I could somehow change that, break the pattern, and raise our child to be a good son or daughter with a heart of benevolence.

Along the way, though, I decided that I can't do so and continue to live at the estate. I have to physically break free from the toxicity that manifested there. Too much blood has been shed for me to forget my purpose in this master plan. How many more secrets lie within the walls of that place that I am unaware of?

No. I can't take anymore. I need to start anew. I will die trying.

"Mrs. Sullivan, are you all right?" the doctor asks.

"No," I whisper, looking at the ground.

"No? Is it the baby?"

Shit. Get it together, Grace.

I straighten myself up and look at his eyes, "I- I mean, yes. I'm sorry. I thought you asked something else."

"It quite all right. Lack of sleep during pregnancy can play some funny tricks on the mind after a while. Come. Follow me this way."

CHAPTER
26

After Dr. Fontenot examines me, I ask to use the ladies' room. Dr. Fontenot clears off the table of the array of instruments he probed me with today.

"It's down the hallway on the right by the staircase. Do you need me to call my butler to show you the way?"

"No, thank you. I should be able to figure it out. Thank you for your services, Dr. Fontenot."

"You're welcome. I know that these examinations can be unpleasant, but I need to do what is best for you and your baby."

"I understand."

He nods farewell, and I smile on my way out the door. I don't stop. I don't stop at the bathroom. I don't stop when the butler says goodbye to me. I don't stop when I reach the front doors. I don't stop as I make my way down the stairs and out onto the street.

I walk quickly north to the train stop. Every minute counts. I think about the train and hope that Hanna was able to buy our two tickets. I think about the multiple lives I'm leaving behind—my strawberry plantation, being a daughter, being a prisoner and a harlot. I start to shed those layers with every minute that passes by.

Until I hear it. It's not the noise of the train. It's something, or *someone*, else.

"Where do ya think ya goin', bitch?"

I halt dead in my tracks. *How is this possible?* I want to turn around and face the person wearing his signature blue bandana who will stop my dream from becoming a reality. I know if I do, then this is real. I can't accept this yet. I cannot fail.

I lift my head and see the church steeple in front of me. I'm so close. *Dear God, help me. I'm so close.*

The train station is right next to the church, just like the doctor told me at my last visit. The train waits for the three o'clock passengers to board. The passengers arriving from New Orleans exit. Commotion is in the air—the train smoke, the people, the hustle and bustle of organized chaos.

It's right there in front of me. *Right here.* I can't stop. So I don't. I need to find Hanna.

"Ya can' leave. He won' let ya. I know ya hear me, bitch!"

I ignore his idle threats. Neither of them can stop me. I pick up my garb and run down the path that crosses in front the church. I can smell the train exhaust piping out of the smokestack as the engines begin to crank up.

I see Hanna. She steps out in front of a pole. I think our eyes meet, but in a flash, she's gone. My view of her is blocked, this time by a familiar horse carriage. *Henry's* horse carriage.

No!

I slow down and come to a standstill in front of his coach. I have nowhere else to run. All I can do is stare at the carriage and pray it isn't Henry inside.

"I tol' ya he won' let ya leave. Now Imma sure he's gonna punish ya."

Will is right. I'll never leave. What was I thinking? The carriage door opens. All hope is definitely lost.

Henry is livid. I've never seen him look so angry, not even when he found me at the secret cottage. I cower backward, until I bump up against Will, who grabs my arms and wraps them around my back.

Henry stalks up to me. I begin to open my mouth to apologize, hoping to calm him down a little. He erases my words with a hard backhanded slap to the face.

God that hurt!

I forgot. It's been so long since anyone put their hands on me like that. My cheek burns, and my head radiates with pain. I blink a few times, to clear my vision, and straighten my posture. I try to speak when Henry issues another backhanded slap in the other direction.

"Ahhh!!" Tears well in my eyes again, and I look down at the ground while Will keeps hold of my hands behind my back.

"Look at me!" Henry bellows.

"No!" My jaw hurts so damn bad. But there is no way in hell I'm going to look at him when all he does is hit me.

"I said look at me!" Spittle flies from his lips.

Will twists my arms harshly, and I cry out in pain. My chest puffs out, and my head raises instinctively. My arms feel like they are about to pop out of socket.

Henry grabs my neck. "Why did you do this to me?!"

The church bell rings, drowning out any reply I might have made. None of my reasons will be good enough for him.

"You betrayed me!" He punches my face with his fist. Pain explodes behind my eyes, and I fall to the asphalt. Not even Will could keep me upright with that blow. I lay in front the church steps grabbing my belly in case Henry, or Will for that matter, try to kick my stomach.

"I knew you were up to something. Ever since you asked me about the train on our way back from McComb the first time. I knew you were looking for an escape route. This train would be your only hope."

The church bell rings for a second time.

"I hoped that when you found out you were pregnant with our child, that you wouldn't care about escaping anymore. We would build the empire you told me you wished to run with me one day. Remember that? That day, I shot and killed your precious *boyfriend*."

How could I forget? A part of me died inside that day.

"But when we visited the doctor and you asked to return to McComb for the next appointment coincidentally at the same time when your escape route is supposed to arrive and leave, I knew you were playing me. You solidified it when you wanted to bring Hanna, your accomplice."

Where is Hanna? The church bell rings finally for the third time. Three o'clock. My time is up. The conductor blows the train horn, signaling its upcoming departure. The loud noise so close overpowers all the surrounding noises, except for my beating heart.

Henry crouches down next to me. He touches my face tenderly. "When I fetched Hanna to tell her that she was expected to ride with us, I decided to also fetch Will. I explained to Will my suspicions and to take his own carriage after we left in case you decided to flee." His light touch morphs into a grip that tightens. "Unfortunately, I was right."

He squeezes my face with one hand.

"When Will saw Hanna leave the doctor's house, he came and found me. Luckily, I got to you just in time. You won't screw this up for me. My legacy needs to continue. You will be a prisoner again in your own room and watched like a hawk so you cannot harm yourself or my baby. Then after you give me what I want, I'll be done with you, for good."

He shoves me away before standing to loom over me.

"Will, get her out of my sight. Tie her up, and ride back with her to the estate. If she does anything or even makes a sound, remind her who is in charge."

"Sho will, boss."

I want to scream and cry, but there is no point. I lose, just like Charles months ago.

Another train horn blasts in the air. Henry turns back to his carriage, and Hanna steps out from behind the carriage, swinging some sort of pipe. She knocks Henry to the ground next to me.

"What ya doin', Hanna?" Will asks, dumbfounded.

I kick Will's legs out from under him and scurry to the side. My head hurts, and I feel disoriented. Will tries to grab me, but I kick my heel in his face, rendering him unconscious.

"Stay on the ground, bitch," I curse. I won't let him lay another finger on me again.

"All aboard!" The conductor yells. Hanna runs over to me with both tickets in hand.

"Take 'em, chil'."

"You're coming with me, right?"

"I can' go. Imma make sure they don' come lookin' for ya."

"Hanna..."

"Go!"

I don't want Hanna to stay behind, but I need to leave. I grab her hands and look at her, "Thank you."

Then, I run as fast as I can.

"Last call! All aboard!"

I reach the train and show my ticket to the conductor. He checks it and points for me to take a seat.

I glance back behind me, at everything, my past. I am only taking what I currently carry. I rest my hands on my belly and find a seat in the train car.

As we depart, I watch the town of McComb blur in the distance. I didn't get the full revenge I wanted for myself, my parents, Charles, and the other prisoners. I may not have killed Henry, but I escaped.

I rub my growing belly gently and know that I will take care of my baby, no matter what. I now think about my future with excitement for new beginnings. A slow smile spreads across my face.

I boarded the train minutes ago headed to somewhere. The conductor says for Chicago. I say for freedom.

ACKNOWLEDGMENTS

I'd like to say a special thank you to a few people who made this book come to life:

To my husband who inspired me to write down my thoughts, no matter how long it took, and for your continued support throughout this journey. I appreciate the joy you shared with me in creating this book.

To my children, who allowed Mommy to write at every chance I could spare and are proud of what I have accomplished. I love you both so deeply.

To my friend, Christy Carpenter, who took me seriously and helped me expand my ideas. I appreciate your alpha reader talents and reading all my drafts, no matter how many times I asked.

To Rebecca Taylor, who gave me the confidence and urged me to move forward with my dream. Thanks to you, I did not put my pen to rest.

To Heather Preis, who took a chance on me and allowed this manuscript to fly without limitations and make my dreams of becoming an author a reality. I cannot thank you enough for allowing a light-hearted conversation turn into a lovely working relationship. I look forward to our future projects.

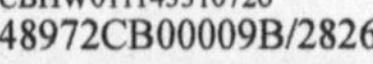